NATIVE ROOTS

A ZEB HANKS MYSTERY SERIES NOVELLA

MARK REPS

This book is a work of fiction. Names and characters are products of the author's imagination. Any similarities between the good people of southeastern Arizona and tribal members of the San Carlos Indian Reservation are purely coincidental.

NATIVE ROOTS

ALSO BY MARK REPS

ZEB HANKS MYSTERY SERIES

NATIVE BLOOD

HOLES IN THE SKY

ADIÓS ÁNGEL

NATIVE JUSTICE

NATIVE BONES

NATIVE WARRIOR

NATIVE EARTH

NATIVE DESTINY

NATIVE TROUBLE

NATIVE ROOTS (PREQUEL NOVELLA)

THE ZEB HANKS MYSTERY SERIES 1-3

AUDIOBOOK

NATIVE BLOOD

HOLES IN THE SKY

ADIÓS ÁNGEL

OTHER BOOKS

BUTTERFLY (WITH PUI CHOMNAK)

HEARTLAND HEROES

PART I

1

ROUGHLY 30 YEARS AGO

12:01 A.M., JULY 4

"Wake up!"

With a great deal of effort, a sleepy thirteen-year-old Zeb Hanks slowly opened his right eye. His left eye felt like it was glued shut. The sandman had obviously paid him a visit. Using the tip of his finger, Zeb dug the crusty sleep from his eyes.

The command to 'wake up' had come from Noah. Despite his somnambulant state, Zeb recognized his brother's voice. Three years older than Zeb, Noah was as used to barking orders at his younger brother as Zeb was hearing them. Zeb assumed the voice was coming from Noah's room, down the hall. Zeb, even in his half-awake state, feared their father would be awakened by the noise. Waking his father would mean a beating for both of them. Once again, the order to wake up groggily entered Zeb's ears. This time Noah's words were accompanied by a punch to his younger brother's arm.

"Wake the hell up!"

"Ow. Crap. Dang it all. Is the house on fire or something?" asked Zeb

"Duh, we're camping in the backyard, you doofus."

Zeb lifted his arm out of his sleeping bag and ran a solitary finger against the canvas side of the tent. Reality came rushing back to him. He and Noah were in the tent in the backyard because they had a plan. Well, truth be told, Noah had the plan. Zeb was the unwitting but available accomplice.

"Don't do that," barked Noah. "Remember dad told us that touching the canvas would cause the tent to leak if it rained."

It had not rained in months. When it did rain, it was a 'dry rain' that evaporated before it touched the ground. Zeb and Noah believed this peculiar phenomenon only occurred in the part of the desert where they lived. Zeb, even half alert, remembered Noah had touched the side of the tent last time it rained. Although it didn't cause the tent to leak, their dad had given Noah a willow branch whipping for what he called 'just being plain stupid'.

Just off the patio, in the backyard of the Hanks' house, was a small patch of grass. It was just large enough to pitch a two-man pup tent. Having grass yards was all the rage in Safford that summer. It was a real status symbol and a brand-new thing to Noah and Zeb. Most of their yard was dirt, strewn periodically with rocks. Larger rocks were piled in the corners, noting the property boundaries. A row of flowers edged the eastern and northern sides of the one-story, three-bedroom rambler.

"It's the fourth of July," said Noah. "Remember our deal?"

Zeb closed his eyes and exhaled loudly. How he wished that he had not exchanged a pinky finger grasp with Noah. The joining of little fingers for this occasion was no different than the time they had cut themselves to become blood brothers, just like the Indian kids did. A deal like they had made must move forward. The consequences of welshing on such a thing would do nothing but create bad juju and disrupt the order of the world the young boys lived in. More than likely it would also lead to a fistfight.

"Get dressed."

"I am dressed," replied Zeb.

"Slept in your clothes, too, huh? Good thinking."

"Are there any lights on in the house?"

"No. I already checked three times."

"Shit."

Zeb swore because lights would have meant the mission was canceled.

"Tough guy, eh," said Noah.

"Whaddaya mean?" asked Zeb.

"I never heard you swear before, little bro."

"Screw you. I swear all the time. I like to swear. Sometimes I swear like a drunken sailor."

Zeb was lying. He didn't swear, well hardly ever. This one just sort of slipped out. His Mormon upbringing had taught him it was a sin to swear. But Zeb also knew there was more to life and religion than the Mormon teachings he had been taught in Sunday school. His mother had recently exposed him to a completely different view of God and religion. She had been taking him to tent revival meetings. These Pentecostal gatherings dwelt heavily on the importance of never taking the name of the Lord in vain. Yet, sometimes when people spoke in tongues, it sounded an awful lot like swear words to Zeb. In his mind there was plenty of room for the justification of swearing. He would be fourteen on his next birthday. That would practically make him a man. Men could swear. Such was the method of his boyish logic.

Zeb's mother, Marta Hanks, took Zeb to these Pentecostal meetings without telling her husband, Jonas. She also never mentioned a word of it to Noah. She implied that Zeb should tell no one, not even his brother. This was strictly a mother-son secret pact involving only Zeb and his mother. Recently they had seen a snake handler at one of the revival meetings that had been held on the Rez. The Pentecostal handler claimed he would never die from a rattlesnake bite because he never broke any of the commandments, did not imbibe in the drinking of demon rum or speak sinfully. That sort of thinking took hold in Zeb's young brain.

"You lie like a rug, little brother, you lie, you lie, you lie."

Noah was of course referring to swearing. Zeb was ticked off. He really wanted to tell Noah to go f*** himself, but young Zeb had already accidentally sworn. Saying what he was thinking was out of the question. The mere idea of spending an eternity in hell shook Zeb to his core.

"Come on. Be quiet. We don't want to wake up Mom and Dad," said Noah.

Even though he wasn't all in on his older brother's plan, there was little if anything Zeb could do to stop it at this point. He glanced up at the midnight sky. It was bursting with a billion beautiful stars. Thankfully, the moon was a waxing crescent moon and half hidden behind Mount Graham. The darkness would help them stay unseen.

"Think we can pull this off without getting caught?" asked Zeb.

"Hell yes, you little chicken shit. Of course we can."

Zeb hated it when his brother called him a chicken shit.

"Am not," blurted Zeb.

"Are too."

"Am not."

Noah egged him on.

"Am not what? Am not what? Say it, Zeb. Say chicken shit. You don't dare because you don't really swear."

Noah put his thumbs in his armpits and began to prance around and squawk like a chicken. Zeb pushed him hard. Noah slugged him in the arm and laughed. Zeb's arm ached, but he refused to give his brother any satisfaction by rubbing away the pain.

Zeb went out of his way to avoid risk and danger. In contrast, Noah thrived on the most perilous of situations. Zeb would never admit it aloud, but his brother's adventures scared the crap out of him. Boys being boys and brothers being brothers, it was a fear he could never let Noah see. If he did appear panicked or frightened, his brother would beat on him.

"We're GONNA get caught. I just know it."

Noah grabbed Zeb by the collar and stared cold and hard into his brother's eyes.

"Shut up or you'll be eating a knuckle sandwich with all the trimmings."

Zeb was certain Noah believed he was a sissy. Zeb had made it to thirteen, almost fourteen, before the first swear word passed through his lips. He had never stolen anything or puffed on a cigarette. Never once did young Zebulon Hanks shirk his duties around the house. He never sneaked out of church or missed Sunday school classes. Noah, on the other hand, always had a pack of cigarettes stashed away, skipped out on Sunday school whenever he could, was a regular cat burglar and swore like a sailor on shore leave. Zeb was pretty sure his brother had even kissed a girl. Maybe he had even gotten to second base, whatever that meant.

"Are you sure we should be doing this?"

Zeb wondered why on earth he had agreed to Noah's risky and perilous plan.

"It's a rite of passage," explained Noah. "You know what that is, right?"

"Yeah," replied Zeb.

Noah was mimicking his father's words who frequently bragged about his own childhood rituals. Maybe this was one of those moments. Maybe Zeb was afraid of disappointing his older brother. The thought suddenly occurred to him that maybe he was becoming the kind of kid who went along with things he didn't believe in. Both the Mormon Bishop Behunin and the Most High Reverend Hensle Wendt, the snake handling clergyman, had warned about such things being almost inevitable if a person did not allow for the presence of the Holy Spirit to reside within. That thing, whatever it was, that made up his conscience was now giving Zeb Hanks a good going over. Zeb listened to that voice until his mind quieted. When it became still, a silent, seething rage grew toward his older brother. Zeb was stuck in the muck and mire of brotherhood. There was literally nothing he could do to alter his fate. He remembered the Pentecostal minister saying that there would be times of trial when one was caught between the devil and the deep blue sea. Zeb knew the darker angels commanded this battle that was going on in his head. Noah's voice interrupted his thoughts.

"I hid the bikes."

"Okay."

Zeb, feeling helpless and ashamed, shivered with bad conscience.

Noah had carefully concealed the bikes in the bushes behind the old shed at the corner of the back yard. Silently Zeb and Noah walked their matching red and black Soaring Eagle Hiawatha bikes down the soft dirt alley. When Noah was certain their parents could neither see nor hear them, he gave the order.

"Let's ride 'em, cowboy. Saddle up."

"If Dad finds out what we're up to, he's gonna beat us," said Zeb.

"I know. So what? It wouldn't be the first and it won't be the last."

"You don't care, do you?"

"Nope. Why should I? I'm gonna get it one way or the other anyway."

To Noah it was just another in a long line of whuppings. The pain he could take. The way Noah had it figured was that maybe it was his dad's only way to show that he cared.

"How can you not worry about getting the tar beat out of you by Dad?" asked Zeb.

"He's gonna find a reason to kick my ass no matter what I do. I don't have Mom protecting me like you do, you little pussy," replied Noah.

Zeb snarled under his breath at his brother making sure he couldn't hear him.

"I'm not a pussy. You're a prick."

Secure in the fact that they were in no immediate danger of getting caught by their father, the boys pedaled aggressively down the street and away from their house. With Noah in the lead, they rode down the alley directly to the abandoned railway station building.

The long-deserted Union Pacific station was a huge, dilapidated, one-story building with faded orange paint and broken windows that were all covered with crisscrossed 2x8 pine boards. The doors were old and easily enough jimmied open with little more than the screwdriver Noah had slipped into his sock. A minute later the boys were inside the dusty old building. A solitary street light created ghostly images across the walls and floor of the decrepit structure.

Noah flipped on his military-style flashlight. Noah had stashed his fireworks in the middle room under some cardboard and other rubble,.

"Nearly a hundred dollars' worth of fireworks," bragged Noah. "Big ones. Great big ones. Practically rockets."

Zeb had no clue how Noah had raised the money to buy the contraband. Noah only made three and half dollars a week on his paper route. He spent most of that on pop, candy and dirty magazines from Schmeers Drug Store. Zeb suspected Noah had bought the fireworks from Red Parrish. Around the fourth of July and New Year's Eve, Red sold them, illegally, out of the back of his bar, Red's Roadhouse. Red was a mean man. Just the sight of him scared Zeb half to death. Somehow his brother was not the least bit afraid of the creepy bar owner.

"Come on, get moving," urged Noah. "The cops could show up any minute."

Zeb's heart pounded like a drum against the inside of his rib cage. His voice, in the process of passing through puberty, squeaked out a high-pitched reply followed by a second one which was baritone in nature.

"I'm coming. I'm coming."

"You pussy. You sound like a girl."

"Bite me," murmured Zeb ever so quietly.

"What?"

"Nothin'," replied Zeb. "At least nothin' that would interest you."

Noah tossed a handful of fireworks into Zeb's arms. He quickly gathered up the rest. The brothers ran at full speed to their bikes. They loaded the fireworks into the side baskets. Zeb's heightened senses intuited danger lurking around every corner. Each shadowy movement in the vacant building increased the intensity of his fear. Zeb glanced over at his older brother. Noah acted as cool as a cucumber. Even though Zeb didn't know what the expression 'as cool as a cucumber' meant, it seemed to fit Noah who carried on as though he didn't have a care in the world.

Through Zeb's eyes, Noah seemed prepared for any possibility that might arise. Zeb knew Noah had spent a great deal of time plotting out this night in his head. He had gone so far as sketching it out on paper. He had brought up his plan a hundred times over. As much as Noah had talked about it and shared many parts of the scheme with Zeb, he also kept many things a secret. Not knowing exactly what was about to happen made Zeb feel even more anxious.

With baskets full of illegal fireworks, they entered Phase two. Noah called it the Kit Carson part of the plan. Kit had worked as an Indian agent in the area a hundred years earlier and was a legend in the boys' mind. Tonight, they were scouts, much like Kit Carson was for the Hudson Bay Company back in the days when the west was truly wild. Checking for danger was their mission. The bad guys, which meant Sheriff Jake Dablo, one of his deputies or some honest citizen of Safford, could pop up just about anywhere.

"Let's cruise by the sheriff's office," said Noah.

Zeb knew that the reason they had ridden within eyeshot of the sheriff's office was to make sure no one was on duty. The office was deserted. Noah spoke again.

"Now we ride by Sheriff Dablo's house. I wanna make sure he is sound asleep, or at least that there are no lights on."

"Gotcha," replied Zeb. "Makes sense."

They zipped through the darkened streets of Safford, staying in the shadows whenever possible. Eventually they rode right past Sheriff Dablo's house.

"The coast is clear."

Noah laughed and spoke with such bravado that the angst and fear momentarily fled from Zeb's heart, mind and body.

"Time to begin celebrating the fourth of July like our forefathers intended. Blowing off some fireworks on this hallowed day is practically our sacred, patriotic duty."

A frightened but exhilarated Zeb could hardly argue with such sound logic.

2

12:33 A.M., JULY 4

Noah growled at Zeb as they sped through the ever-darkening streets of Safford.

"Move it, pokey man."

"I don't want to hit a pot hole."

"Baby."

"Up yours."

"The first thing we should do is blow up the bathrooms at the park."

"Why?" asked Zeb.

"Cuz I said so. It's part of the master plan."

"How are we going to do that with these fireworks?"

"Jesus, but you're a numb nuts. I got some M-80s," replied Noah. They're waterproofed. They're made for blowing up toilets. Everybody knows that."

"Where'd you get them? You can't buy them in town. They're double illegal in Arizona."

Zeb figured one of Noah's friends who had a driver's license had made a little trip to Mexico where supposedly the bigger stuff could be had cheaply.

"I suppose I can tell you. But you keep your mouth shut about it or somebody might cut your tongue out."

Noah stuck out his tongue and pretended to slice it with a knife. Zeb knew his older brother was just acting like a tough guy with such a stupid threat. People only did that kind of thing in the movies they showed at the drive-in theater.

"Where'd you get M-80s? It's a three hundred dollar fine if you get caught with them," said Zeb. "I've heard you go to jail if they catch you blowing them up."

"We ain't gonna get caught then, are we?"

Noah pulled into an alley. Zeb was right behind him.

"I got 'em from Red's kid, Red Junior. You know who he is?"

"Yeah. He's got a screw loose if you ask me."

"Who's askin' ya?"

"Just sayin'."

"If you tell anyone and Red Junior finds out, he'll beat the crap out of me. If he beats the crap out of me, I'm going to beat the tar out of you. Got it?"

Zeb wasn't up for a beating. His brother had pounded on him regularly enough as it was. He had no intention of getting a hard beating that would be the end result of telling anyone about Red Jr.

"My lips are sealed."

Zeb ran his thumb and first finger across his lips and turned an imaginary key, the universal indicator that his lips were truly sealed.

"They'd better be."

Noah headed out of the alley and back onto the street.

"How are we going to blow up the toilets?" asked Zeb.

"All we gotta do is toss the M-80s down the shitter and blammo —destroyed."

"Why are we gonna do that?" asked Zeb.

"Ray Deyo," replied Noah.

"Ray Deyo?"

"Yup. Ray Deyo."

"What do you have against him? He's just a poor, crippled-up city worker," said Zeb. "He's got a lousy enough job keeping the toilets clean. Why make his life even worse?"

Noah reached over and smacked Zeb hard on the back of his head.

"You stupid or what?"

"Or what, I guess," said Zeb, rubbing his sore skull.

"Don't back talk me," ordered Noah.

"I still don't get it."

"Remember when I got grounded for two weeks last summer?"

"Yeah. You and those dorky friends of yours wrote graffiti all over town. That was stupid. You shoulda' known you couldn't get away with it. Especially since you did it while it was still daylight out."

"Shut your trap," said Noah. "It was Ray Deyo who ratted me out to Sheriff Dablo. This is about revenge for the beating I got from the old man because gimpy Ray's got a big mouth."

"You guys were stupid to put your initials on the graffiti," said Zeb.

"Ray Deyo shouldn't have ratted us out. It's practically a law that you don't fink on other guys. It's what they call a code. Yeah, the code of silence."

Zeb had watched in terror as their father beat his brother with a belt because Ray Deyo had told him about the graffiti. Under Ray's watchful eye it took Noah only ten minutes of painting to cover the graffiti he had sprayed on the walls. Zeb had watched him repair the damage. Every memory he had of what happened made Zeb squeamish.

The graffiti Noah and his friends had written on the walls at the park was practically an American tradition. The had defaced the biffy walls and four or five other walls on businesses with colorful Krylon paint. They aerosol sprayed the same sayings kids did every year; *Kilroy was here. Safford Rules!! Jim Morrison lives! Smoke Pot!* Besides the usual sayings, Noah and his pals had left their initials behind. In this moment, in the middle of the night on July 4th, when he and his brother were about to blow up the park toilets, the graffiti didn't seem like much of an offense at all.

"I think you didn't deserve the beating Dad gave you," said Zeb.

"Aw, it was nothin'," replied Noah. "He's beat me worse than that."

"When?" asked Zeb.

"One time when you were at church camp. I stole some money from his pocketbook when he was drunk. Twenty bucks. He beat me so bad Mom almost had to take me to the hospital. Dad wouldn't let her. I still got a lump on the back of my head. Here, feel it."

Zeb ran his fingers over a large lump on the back of his brother's head.

"Dad did that? With his hand? With a belt?"

"Naw. He hit me with 34-ounce Louisville Slugger. It was just a glancing blow. But if I hadn't ducked, I'd probably be dead."

"Geez," said Zeb. "How come you never told me?"

"The old man said if I told anyone, including you, he'd disappear me."

"Disappear you? What's that mean?"

Noah made the image of a knife slicing across his throat.

Zeb gasped.

Then Noah placed his pointer finger against his temple, mimicking being shot.

"No," cried Zeb. "That didn't really happen. Did it?"

"Just tellin' it like it went down."

"Why does Dad hate you so much?" asked Zeb.

"I dunno. I heard him and Mom arguing one time. He said that I didn't look like either of them."

"You look like Grandpa."

"I know. Maybe that's the problem."

"What's that supposed to mean?"

Noah stared his younger, naive brother in the eye.

"You figure it out. Let's get rolling. Time's a wasting," said Noah.

Zeb and Noah headed down a back alley, onto some side streets before ending up within eyeshot of the city park. They stashed their bikes behind some bushes in an unlit area near the Klippel Candy and Flower Shop.

"Time to get even with that crippled old bastard," said Noah.

Zeb felt badly about what they were going to do as they sneaked toward the toilets. Old man Deyo had been injured in the war. He walked with a limp because the Nazis shot him three times in the leg. He was even captured and put into a prison camp where the only food they had was dead mice and insects. Ray had seen more than his fair share of bad times. It was rumored he still had shrapnel from the Nazi bullets in his leg. Still, there was no turning back now. Besides, how much damage could an M-80 do to a toilet anyway?

"You take the women's biffy. I'll take the men's head," said Noah. "You got fire, right?"

Zeb reached into his pocket and pulled out an old Zippo lighter. He'd won it in a marble game. It lit on the first flip. It always did.

"Cool," said Noah.

"What's it look like when a toilet blows up?"

"I dunno. Never done it before," replied Noah.

"How do you know it will work?"

"Shut up."

"Okay."

The brothers stood with their backs flat against the cool cement block wall of the toilet building, scanning their eyes in all directions.

"The coast is clear," said Zeb.

"Check your watch," ordered Noah. "In exactly two minutes light the M-80 and drop it in the toilet. Once it kerplops in the toilet water get the hell out of there. I don't want to be responsible if a flying toilet seat kills you. If that happened, Mom and Dad would both kill me."

Death from a flying toilet seat was one possibility Zeb hadn't even remotely considered. Oddly, as he entered the ladies' bathroom, it became the only thing on his mind. He imagined newspaper head-lines that said, 'Local boy killed by flying toilet seat at city park'. He shook the ridiculous thought from his head and quickly found the toilet. Flipping on his Zippo lighter, Zeb saw a strange white metal container hanging on the wall just above the toilet roll. He checked his watch. Fifty seconds had passed. He had seventy seconds before he would light the M-80. Zeb held his lit Zippo up next to the box. From the corner of his right eye he read some small black lettering on the white metal container. It said 'Do not flush tampons. Place in container.'

What the hell? Do not flush tampons? This was as big of a mystery as what would happen when an M-80 was flushed down a toilet. Zeb had been in many men's rooms. He had never seen the likes of that. He re-checked his watch. Forty-five seconds to detonation. Hmm. All the things he learned at Bible school told him not to lift the lid of the white metal container. The little voice of curiosity, the not so bad devil inside his head, demanded he take a peek. The angel that danced on his other shoulder told him not to have a look. Impish curiosity won the battle.

Zeb lifted the lid and put his lighter by the opening.

"Ick."

It was gross. Something bloody and smelly like fish was in there. He didn't know what the heck it was. Zeb slammed the lid shut. He was angry at himself for looking. He knew he had listened to the wrong voice.

Zeb heard a car in the near distance. A sense of panic set in. Should he light the M-80 now? Did Noah hear the car? Should he call out to his brother? His heart churned like the engine on a car in the Indy 500. Zeb lit the M-80. He dropped it in the toilet. Just as he imagined, it made a 'kerplunk' sound. He froze. Two seconds later he heard a booming sound from the men's room. Noah had blown his M-80 early. Zeb's blew five seconds later. Water and small bits of busted plastic toilet seat flew everywhere.

Noah and Zeb practically ran over each other as they raced out of the toilets to their bikes. Both were laughing like hyenas. At that moment Zeb realized he was uncertain as to exactly how hyenas laughed. On the other hand, he was absolutely certain that he and Noah were doing a perfect imitation.

"Let's get the hell out of here," said Noah. "I think that was Sheriff Dablo driving by."

"Shit."

"Potty mouth," said Noah with all the sarcasm he could muster.

3

1:15 A.M., JULY 4

Noah and Zeb raced to the Klippel Candy and Flower Shop where they had stashed their bikes in some bushes. Their hiding spot gave them a perfect view of Main Street. It was all part of Noah's plan.

"We've got to watch to see if Sheriff Dablo is patrolling. We have to see how often he passes through the downtown area."

"But we know his lights are out and that his car is at his place," said Zeb.

"If you were the sheriff, wouldn't you have a peek around town as it neared midnight?"

"Yeah, I suppose I would," replied Zeb. "Makes sense. Everyone knows troublemakers show up around midnight."

It dawned on Zeb that when he and Noah watched detective movies, Noah was watching the bad guys, while he was watching the good guys. Noah knew all the fine details of criminal activity. It now appeared his older brother had studied the criminal mind as well. From watching the good guys, Zeb knew that Sheriff Dablo, if he were out and about, would make the rounds one or two times then head back home. Tomorrow was the 4th of July, a big day in Safford. Sheriff Dablo and his deputies would have to keep order, direct traffic, make sure the parade route flowed evenly and even ride in the parade while periodically blowing off their sirens. Those were the things that came immediately to Zeb's mind. He was certain there were at least a dozen responsibilities on such an important day. Zeb knew they were safe. He knew the best plan would be to scope out the sheriff's house again by sneaking down a couple of back streets. But Zeb wasn't going to tell Noah that, because he wasn't in on Phase two of his brother's plan.

"Time for Phase Two," said Noah.

"What's Phase Two?" asked Zeb.

"It involves old man Klippel, owner of the Klippel Candy and Flower Shop."

"He's a pretty good guy. A couple of times when I didn't have enough money for candy, Mr. Klippel gave me the candy on credit."

"He hates my guts," said Noah.

Zeb knew exactly what Noah was talking about.

"He caught me stealing candy a few times."

"More like ten times," said Zeb. "And the first six or seven times he didn't even do anything to you."

"Shut your yap."

"Well..."

"But I owe him cause of Mom."

"Mom?"

"Yeah. I was picking up a dozen roses and a large box of chocolates for her birthday, but I forgot to pay for them."

Zeb witnessed the entire event. He was riding his bicycle when he saw Mr. Klippel chasing Noah out the door of his store and down Main Street. Noah had ditched the flowers just outside the front door as soon as he figured out Mr. Klippel was after him. He opened the candy box, grabbed a few pieces, then dumped the rest all over the sidewalk. Less than fifty feet after ditching the candy, Klippel caught up with Noah and grabbed him by the collar. He hauled him right over to Sheriff Dablo's office. The sheriff called Zeb and Noah's parents. Not only was it embarrassing, but everyone in town seemed to hear about it within a day. Marta felt so horrible she didn't even want to go to Sunday church service for the next month. Jonas, who didn't regularly attend services, didn't really care what people thought and marched Noah and Zeb right down to the front pew. At Sunday dinner when Marta was fretting about what people would say, Jonas simply said, "Let them talk." And talk many people did. After Sunday lunch, Jonas took Noah out behind the garage and gave him the belt, once for each rose and twice for the box of candy.

But now things had changed. Klippel was in Noah's crosshairs. To get even with the candy man, Noah's plan was to have both he and Zeb toss M-80s and cherry bombs into the dumpster behind his business. This would create a mess of so-called 'epic proportions' according to Noah.

When Noah decided the coast was clear, the boys hopped on their bikes and headed for the dumpster.

"Got your Zippo handy?"

"Yeah."

"Then get your cherry bombs and M-80s ready."

All at once the fear that had been coursing through Zeb's veins disappeared. He remembered a saying that he thought fit the situation, *In for a penny, in for a pound.* Once again, he only half understood what it meant, but knowing there was no turning back, he answered like a wartime pilot, "Roger that."

Noah loved the authority, the power and the bravado.

"Over and out."

Rounding a corner onto Third Street, Zeb and Noah simultaneously slammed on their brakes when they spotted a commotion near Klippel's dumpster. Since it was happening after midnight, it was highly suspicious activity. The boys quickly dismounted their bikes. They hid themselves behind the corner building and stared down the alley. Their hawkish eyes set their sights on what was happening. It was dark, too dark to see clearly. Zeb was certain he saw three men. Two of the men were hitting the third man. They were hitting him real hard. Zeb could tell by the ugly sounds he was hearing. It looked like they were hitting him with a big stick or a baseball bat. Zeb immediately thought of the thirty-four-ounce Louisville Slugger his dad had used on his brother's head when Noah had stolen twenty dollars from his wallet. Strangely, the man being beaten made no sound whatsoever. The only noise that could be heard was the grunting of the men doing the beating and the dull thud of wood against clothing.

"What can you see?" whispered Zeb.

"Somebody is taking a beating. That's for sure."

"The man getting beaten up has long hair, down to his shoulders."

"I'd guess he's an Apache."

"One of the guys smacking him around has a ponytail. I bet he's an Apache too."

"The third dude has a cowboy hat on," said Noah.

Zeb squinted as he stared at the cowboy hat. Something about it seemed familiar.

A block away a car made a turn. Its headlights shot some beams on the men.

"The Indian taking the beating has tattoos on his arms," said Zeb.

"That's not tattoos. That's blood," replied Noah.

The time of night, lack of moonlight and poor lighting made it impossible to tell if it was blood or tattoos.

"I can't tell for sure," said Zeb. "It's too dark."

Then, as the larger of the two men who were doing the beating came down hard with his weapon, Zeb and Noah could see in the distant, dim ray of a streetlight that the weapon was indeed shaped like a baseball bat. The final blow landed with a sickening crunch. Zeb was absolutely certain bones had been broken.

"She-it, did you hear that?" asked Noah.

The poor fellow who was taking the beating crumpled in a heap.

Zeb felt like vomiting. Noah watched with wonder as the pony-tailed Indian spat and growled at the man he was beating.

"Get up you son of a bitch. Get up. What you did deserves more of a beating than you're taking."

Zeb could tell from the inflection that he was an Indian. If indeed he was an Indian, it was a near certainty he was Apache. His earlier assumptions had been correct.

The downed, flattened man, at least in Zeb's eyes, was in no condition to move. He wondered why the man who was beating him was demanding that he stand up just to take more of a beating.

"Goddamn coward," shouted the Indian. "You can break a boy's heart, but you can't take a straight on beating, can you? This is a lesson that you won't soon forget, unless you're an absolute idiot."

By now Zeb and Noah's eyes had adjusted to the dark. With the help of a distant streetlight, they could see reasonably well. The man who had just been cracked, either on the head or over the back, just laid there not moving a muscle. He didn't utter as much as a groan. The silence was eerily deafening. Even from a distance and in the darkness, Zeb was certain the man was bleeding badly. In Zeb's mind the thoroughly beaten Indian might even be dead.

"I think he's a goner," whispered Zeb.

"Naw. I've been beaten enough times to know he ain't dead. He's hurtin', that's for certain. But he's still got life left in him."

Noah was speaking from experience. The two men who had done the thrashing stood there, hovering like death itself over the doomed man. The world, in that alley behind the stores, was as quiet as church on a Thursday morning. The beaters stood over the whipped man, glaring at him with hatred.

"He's gotta be dead," said Zeb, holding a hand to the side of his mouth.

"Maybe they're just taking a break," whispered Noah, remembering how his dad got winded beating him. "It takes a lot of strength to give a whupping like that."

"I hope they're done," said Zeb softly.

"Hard to say. Thumpers like it when they get a second wind."

"Let's get the heck outta here..."

Zeb's words were interrupted by a loud sneeze that came from Noah. Zeb saw that his older brother had tried to muffle his nose with his hand. He didn't see any snot on his brother's hand. He figured it was a dry sneeze. Still, it was loud. The men turned in Zeb and Noah's direction.

"Don't move," whispered Noah.

Zeb froze into a statue. Noah, crouching behind Zeb, reached out and grabbed his younger brother by the collar. He spoke in an even lower whisper.

"Not a single muscle. Got it?"

"Yeah."

"They can't see us because there's no light behind us. If we move, they'll be able to tell where we are."

Zeb was too frightened to move. The men took two steps in the boys' direction. Then they simply stopped. The man in the cowboy hat grabbed the ponytailed man by the shoulder. Zeb and Noah could hear the men exchanging words but couldn't make out what they were saying. The men remained frozen. The boys made no more movement than a pair of graveyard headstones. From the little light that was present, Zeb could see clearly that the men were staring in his and Noah's direction. An incredibly long minute passed. It seemed to be an eternity as another minute slowly passed. Zeb was certain the men could hear his heart beating. Eventually they turned away from Zeb and Noah's direction.

"Let's get the hell out of here," said the man in the cowboy hat.

The other man grunted something incomprehensible.

The big men each bent near the body, one by the feet, the other by the head. The Indian was near the feet. The man in the cowboy hat was near the head. The Indian was doing something with the man's boots. Zeb couldn't tell what he was doing, but in the end it looked like he tossed the man's boots at the dumpster. After a couple of minutes, the beaters grabbed the man, and grunted loudly as they tossed the body into the back of the pickup truck.

"They're treating him like he's a piece of meat," said Zeb.

"Yeah," replied Noah. "A carcass."

The man in the cowboy hat had already slid in behind the wheel of the truck. The Indian slammed the tailgate shut then reached over it into the back of the truck. Zeb thought he heard another groan.

The Indian pulled something from his shirt pocket and leaned over where Zeb assumed the man's head was laying. Then the Indian pulled something from his back pocket and lifted up the beaten man's unbooted foot. Zeb heard a crunching, cutting sound. The Indian dropped the foot back inside the back of the truck and began looking on the ground, like he had dropped something.

"Let's get the hell out of here," said the man in the cowboy hat.

Whatever the ponytailed Indian was looking for was quickly forgotten, and he hopped into the cab of the truck. The driver made a U-turn in the alley and the truck slipped off into the dark of night.

"Hmm," said Noah. "Wonder what the hell that was all about?"

Zeb shivered with fear. He had seen enough to know he did not need to know what it was all about.

4

1:30 A.M., JULY 4

Zeb remained frozen, awaiting Noah's command. As he stood there Zeb's mind spun at the speed of a thousand thoughts a second. Death, if indeed they had just witnessed a murder, had come far too close for Zeb's liking. A queasy angst engulfed him. Noah broke the stillness of what had become a silent night.

"That was some badass shit. I think they killed him. Wow! Kind of cool to think we might have just witnessed a murder in the making."

Zeb's heart was racing as fast as his mind. So many questions rushed through his brain. Had they just witnessed a murder? What should they do? Had he put himself in a position for which there was no turning back? Why on earth would Noah think it was cool? He and Noah weren't even supposed to be out at this hour. Horror and dread were only the tip of the iceberg of his utterly confused emotions.

"What are we going to do?" asked Zeb.

"Let me think," replied Noah.

"Well think fast. I don't want to stick around here."

"If we tell the cops what we saw, and they find those guys, we are dead meat," said Noah. "If they killed a man, beat him to death with a baseball bat, they sure wouldn't give a shit about killing a couple of kids. We'd be easy pickins."

"But if they killed a guy and we just saw it, it's our obligation as citizens of Graham County to tell Sheriff Dablo, isn't it?"

"Yeah, right," said Noah.

Zeb, scared to death, did not immediately catch the sarcasm in his brother's voice. He felt an instant moment of relief until Noah spoke again.

"Not even you're that stupid. Jesus H. Christ, sometimes I think you are a full-blown, half-wit window licker."

All at once the old expression Zeb had heard many times, *damned if you do and damned if you don't*, made perfect sense. Zeb knew he and his brother were screwed. That's all there was to it. Out there, in the not so distant future, death's grip may be awaiting them.

"Let's go home and sleep on it," suggested Noah. "It'll look different in the morning."

Zeb couldn't get what he had just seen out of his mind. The whole scene was an instant replay repeated over and over again in his head. How could Noah remain so calm? The beating and its horrible sounds wouldn't stop whirling around inside of Zeb's head. Zeb was deeply lost in that exact thought when Noah grabbed his bicycle handlebar and stopped him cold.

"Wait! Let's at least go have an up-close look at the scene of the crime."

"What? Are you crazy? What if they come back?"

With every fiber of his being Zeb felt certain the bad guys would come back and visit the scene of the crime. Call it instinct. Call it watching bad guy movies. Call it what you will. Zeb knew these evil-doers had just committed a major crime. Zeb's skin tingled with trepidation. His entire body was awash with the bad kind of goosebumps, the kind that come with absolute fright. Returning to the scene of the crime was a risk he did not want to be goaded into.

"Come on. Are you a chicken shit or what?"

Zeb sighed loudly and held his ground.

"Not gonna do it. No way. No how."

"I don't believe it. A Hanks, my brother, is a coward who'd probably desert in war time."

Zeb was outraged. How dare Noah make such a statement. There
were no circumstances where Zeb would allow himself to be branded
as such.

"I guess I'll do it by myself. Wait until your friends hear about
this. They'll call you a gutless wonder, or worse, a girly-boy."

Zeb was trapped by his brother's bullying. Even if Zeb's friends
didn't believe Noah, Noah's friends would make a big production in
front of everyone about Zeb being a coward. Zeb gritted his teeth. His
brother had successfully intimidated him into going against his own
will and better judgement. With great trepidation Zeb followed his
older brother to the scene of the crime. With his eyes darting in every
direction, Zeb was certain that each subtle movement in the darkness
was danger lurking. He knew the bad guys always returned to the
scene of the crime. It was only a question of when, not if.

"What should we do if they come back?" whispered Zeb.

Noah answered with much bravado in his voice.

"You can talk in a normal voice. All is good. We're safe."

"Still, Noah, we have to have a plan if they return."

"For Christ's sake, you know what to do. I swear dealing with you
is like dealing with someone from special class. What the hell do you
think you should do if we run into the bad guys? Huh?!"

"Ride away really fast," blurted Zeb.

"More like ride like your life depends on it. Because it will."

Zeb's heart fluttered at the thought. His bigger, older brother
could most certainly ride faster than he could, if it came down to that.
But, what choice did he have? He was not safe at all, but he considered the fact that he might be safer with his brother than alone, especially if the bad guys saw him. He followed his brother, but not
without great reluctance. Zeb hung his head as he replied.

"Okay, but if we get killed, it's your fault."

"If they come back, we'll have to split up and just get the hell out
of here. You go one way and I'll go the other. If you get caught, don't
be a rat fink. You're better off dead than being a squealer."

Zeb eyeballed the area. He worked up a plan of escape in his head, should it be necessary. This alley was his turf. He knew it like the back of his hand. Noah spent his time in places more hidden than an alley behind Main Street. He hung out in darker, more secret areas where he and his friends could smoke cigs and drink beer, or liquor stolen from their dads' booze bins. Zeb had a weird thought about the time Noah had tried to talk him into smoking a cancer stick. One ciggy butt was all he needed to know it wasn't for him. Never again. Some lessons are learned quickly, others not so fast. Zeb had yet to try drinking a beer even though his brother had bugged him many times to do so. The smell reminded him of his dad when he was drunk. He wanted nothing to do with that. Zeb cleared his head and brought himself back to the task at hand.

Curiosity, he knew, had killed the cat. Zeb figured that meant don't be too curious or you might get in trouble, maybe even end up dead. He was certain he understood that one.

"I don't want to end up killed on the fourth of July," said Zeb. "That would just be plain wrong."

"Then get your escape plan down," warned Noah.

"Already got one."

Zeb had a good getaway plan mapped out in his head. It involved a narrow passageway between the Gamble's store and Drurcks Plumbing and Heating. He had sneaked through there a couple of times when one of Noah's buddies wanted to pound him after he beat him in a game of mumble-de-peg. Zeb was handy with a knife, maybe the best mumble-de-peg player for his age in all of Graham County. He had beaten Noah's friend and won his knife from him. Noah stole the knife from Zeb and gave it back to his friend. In any case, because of mumble-de-peg, he knew how to sneak through that little alley that most everyone just ignored. After that first time when Noah's friend was going to pound him, Zeb returned to the alley and moved some junk out of the way in order to make a clearer path.

Noah and Zeb biked cautiously toward what Zeb was becoming more certain by the second was an actual murder scene. As they neared the area, Zeb noticed a strange feeling. It was almost as if it were alive with the brutal activity that had recently taken place. Zeb would have sworn on a stack of bibles that he could feel the pain of the man who had taken the dreadful beating.

Noah slammed on his brakes and pointed to the ground.

"Good lord. Look at that."

Blood pooled in one distinct area and large, reddish drops were easily seen in another dozen smaller spots. Everything about the place sickened Zeb. He wanted to erase it from his mind. He couldn't. The intensity of the murder zone was the only image his mind's eye could focus on. Years later he would understand this as one of the ways PTSD manifests its brutal face.

Noah surveyed the area with his hands on his hips. He spoke as calmly as Mister Rogers from the TV show.

"Yes, they must have cracked open his skull. Then again once I cut my scalp just a little bit, and that bled something terrible. It was a sight to see."

Zeb nodded, using all his might to suppress his puke reflex. Where would that much blood come from? It seemed extraordinary that so much blood could be in one spot. It reminded Zeb of the time he saw his dad gut a deer that was hanging from a tree in their backyard.

In the next moment, reality zoomed in as a pair of truck head-lamps cloaked the boys in light.

"Shit," they both shouted as they hopped on their bikes.

"Don't follow me," yelled Noah. "Go the other way."

But his older brother was heading directly to the narrow passageway between the Gamble's store and Drurcks Plumbing and Heating. Noah was stealing Zeb's getaway route.

The boys didn't make it twenty feet before a spotlight froze them like deer in the headlights. There was nowhere to turn, nowhere to run and definitely nowhere to hide. They were caught, dead to rights. Zeb looked at Noah. Noah stared at the ground. He carried the look of the defeated on his face. They had some serious explaining to do.

5

1:43 A.M., JULY 4

S heriff Dablo took his time getting out of the cruiser. The boys stood next to their bikes, not moving an inch. For what seemed like an eternity, Zeb felt the heat of the spotlight blazing on them. When Sheriff Dablo removed the powerful light from their faces, he ran it up and down their bodies. Noah spoke quietly to Zeb out of the corner of his mouth.

"He's checking us for weapons."

"Us? We don't carry weapons."

"I've got a knife strapped under my seat," said Noah.

"What?"

Then Zeb remembered he had a pocketknife in his jeans. But that wasn't a weapon, was it?

Their conversation was interrupted when Sheriff Dablo turned off the spotlight, got out of the car and ambled over to the boys. Zeb noticed how big the sheriff suddenly seemed. His size scared Zeb. Sheriff Dablo eyed the Hanks brothers up and down without saying as much as a single word. Eventually, he tipped his cowboy hat back. When he tipped his hat up, Zeb had a dark realization. One of the men doing the beating was wearing a cowboy hat just like the one sitting atop Sheriff Dablo's head. He didn't want to believe it could have been the sheriff who had beaten a man, maybe to death. He shivered involuntarily. The sheriff moved in next to Zeb. When Sheriff Dablo placed a hand on Zeb's shoulder, he jumped.

"You okay, son?"

"Ye-ye-yes, sir. I'm fine," replied Zeb.

"No fun getting caught, is it?"

"No, sir. No fun at all."

Sheriff Dablo gave Zeb another once over. He looked at young Zeb with a sense of compassion. Sheriff Dablo was well aware that Zeb's father was a lifetime, petty criminal as well as a drunk. He also knew Noah was a juvenile delinquent headed down a shady path. Sheriff Dablo assumed Marta Hanks felt powerless to change anything. There was a pretty good chance she had lost her faith. To the sheriff, Zeb was the only hope for the Hanks family. Jake made up his mind right then and there to try and see what he could do to make sure that Zeb followed the straight and narrow path. He knew Song Bird, Medicine Man on the San Carlos reservation, would help him. Sheriff Dablo stopped his musings about the solutions that might come to be and brought himself back to the situation at hand.

"Should have thought about that before you did whatever you did."

Zeb was ready to confess to the toilet destruction. He was smart enough not to mention what he had seen in the alley. For the moment he kept his mouth shut.

"Noah, your behavior doesn't surprise me. You remind me a lot of your old man."

"I ain't nothin' like my old man," snarled Noah.

Sheriff Dablo scoffed loudly enough for the boys to hear.

"Noah, you're old enough to know better. Zeb, you might still be shittin' yellow, but you should be smart enough to know right from wrong."

"Yes, sir," replied Zeb. "I should know right from wrong."

"Shut up," snapped Noah.

"Speak when you're spoken to, Noah," said Sheriff Dablo.

Noah stared down at his shoes.

"Zeb, what the hell are you doing running with your brother at this time of night?"

Sheriff Dablo knew the Hanks family far too well. The sheriff had been called to Zeb's house multiple times. Each time it was for the same thing; a drunken Jonas Hanks was pounding on his wife, Marta Hanks. The same neighbor always called in the complaint. As was typical of spousal abuse, Marta never pressed charges. Sheriff Dablo had picked up Noah for everything from stealing a bike to stealing candy and, of course, there was the graffiti incident. Sheriff Dablo knew everyone in town. He knew the Hanks' household a little too well.

Oddly, Zeb was unexpectedly more exhilarated than nervous. He had witnessed a crime. Now, maybe, just maybe, he could tell someone about it. He would sleep better. That was for certain. It might even put his mind at ease. Zeb wondered what Sheriff Dablo was waiting for. Why wasn't he questioning them? Then he noticed Sheriff Dablo was looking past Noah and peering up and down the alley and into the side streets.

Again, the thought that maybe it was Sheriff Dablo who was in on the beating entered Zeb's mind. Maybe Sheriff Dablo had beaten a man to death, or almost to death, or maybe he hadn't. Maybe the sheriff ended up in the alley because he had gotten a call from a concerned citizen. Lots of men had cowboy hats just like the one that sat on the sheriff's head. Zeb was beginning to breathe easy. Maybe it was all a coincidence. Maybe he and Noah weren't in any real trouble at all. His relief was short-lived.

"Ray Deyo called my house. He got me out of bed. I was sleeping just fine. I didn't feel much like getting out from beneath the sheets when I was sound asleep, and I was sleeping like a lamb," said Sheriff Dablo.

"Nobody likes it when someone wakes them up from sleep," said Zeb.

"Shut your yap," sneered Noah.

"Ray's got insomnia. You boys know what that is?"

Zeb and Noah shook their heads. They had no idea what insomnia was.

"Insomnia means you can't sleep. Not only does Ray have trouble sleeping, he's got a painful bad back. That shrapnel he took from the Nazis robs him of his slumber. That's two good reasons he can't sleep. And, any man who's been a Nazi prisoner of war and tortured probably is haunted by demons you and I can't even imagine."

"That's terrible to think about," said Zeb.

"Yeah," added Noah, who, from watching a lot of WWII movies, hated the Nazis.

"It is too bad," said Sheriff Dablo. "Everyone, especially kids, need to get the right amount of rest."

"I learned that in health class," said Zeb.

Noah sneaked a quick punch to Zeb's kidneys. Zeb didn't understand why.

"Injured war veterans need their rest too. Especially those who gave so much for their country," said Sheriff Dablo.

"Makes sense," said Zeb, preparing his body for another kidney punch.

Noah glared at Zeb as Sheriff Dablo separated the boys to prevent Noah from another physical outburst towards his brother.

"Ray was feeling poorly, restless like he often gets. He couldn't sleep so he got up and decided to drive around. He thought it might make him tired enough to sleep. He was driving by the park and stopped to take a leak. It didn't take him long to see that someone had messed with the toilets. You boys wouldn't happen to know anything about that, would you?"

Before Zeb could even think to answer, the lies flowed out of Noah's mouth like water running over Niagara Falls.

"We were camping out in the backyard and decided to go for a midnight ride," said Noah. "We haven't been anywhere near the park. Have we, Zeb?"

Noah gave Zeb the death stare. No words needed to be spoken. The look told Zeb that Noah would pound him within an inch of his life if he didn't agree with the lie.

"Uh. Huh."

Nothing that passed between the boys had been missed by Sheriff Dablo.

"What do a couple of midnight riders do on the fourth of July?" asked Sheriff Dablo. "Riding and hiding?"

Zeb smiled. Sheriff Dablo was cool enough to make a vague reference to an Allman Brothers song. Zeb had heard it recently on KOMA, a late-night radio station out of Oklahoma City. Maybe, he thought, Sheriff Dablo is really a good guy. Zeb was about to say something when Noah started in again with the lies.

"We were cruising around the alleys looking for tossed out pop bottles. The Thriftee Grocery Store gives us five cents each for them."

Noah paused to giggle before continuing the tall tale he had started.

"We even got these."

Noah pulled some legal ladyfinger firecrackers out of his back pocket.

"We were going to start celebrating a little early by blowing a few off. All in good fun of course. You know, get the dogs all excited and barking."

"Some might call that disturbing the peace," interjected Sheriff Dablo.

"It's all in good fun. Weren't you ever a kid, Sheriff? Besides we were going over to the old abandoned cotton storage plant. Nobody lives over that way. You know that. We thought that blowing up some cotton clumps would look like confetti. Didn't we, Zeb?"

"Yeah," said Zeb. "That's what you told me."

It was then Sheriff Dablo noticed the boys staring at the blood on the ground. The beam from his flashlight shined directly on it. The blood looked like a combination of red mud and shadows. Sheriff Dablo bent down and pressed his fingers into the mess. He rubbed his thumb and first finger together, checking the texture. Then he placed his fingers to his nose. Zeb had never smelled blood on purpose. He wondered if it smelled good or bad. He assumed it smelled like rust because it was red.

"You boys know anything about this blood?"

"Uh, not really."

Zeb found the guts to speak up before any more lies could spew from his brother's mouth.

"Not really? What's that supposed to mean?" asked Sheriff Dablo.

"We saw three men, Sheriff Dablo. Two Indians with long hair. One had a ponytail. The third guy was white. He had on a cowboy hat." Zeb stopped in mid-sentence and pointed to the sheriff's head. "Just like yours."

Sheriff Dablo place his large hand over the top of his cowboy hat and brought it back into its regular position.

"What was going on?"

"One of the Indians, the one in the ponytail, and the guy in the cowboy hat were beating up the other guy. I think they were hitting him with a Louisville Slugger."

"Beating him with a baseball bat?" asked Sheriff Dablo. "That's not good."

"Maybe it was a stick. We were at least a hundred feet away. It was hard to tell. It's awful dark back here in the alley," said Zeb.

"Where were you standing?"

"Over there."

Zeb pointed to the spot. Noah was dead silent.

"Did the men who were doing the beating see you?"

"Maybe," said Zeb. "I don't think so. They might have heard us when Noah sneezed."

Noah gave Zeb a dirty look. Even though they were ten feet apart, Zeb tightened the muscles over his kidneys.

"What'd they do then?"

"The stopped for a minute, then they picked up the beat-up guy and tossed him into the back of their truck," said Zeb.

"Would you recognize the truck?" asked the sheriff.

"It was brown, I think," replied Zeb. "It looks like a hundred other trucks around town."

"Noah? You see the same thing?"

"I didn't really get a good look at the truck."

Zeb knew Noah was lying. He didn't know why, but he would soon.

"Either of you recognize if it was a Ford, Chevy or Dodge? Perhaps the year of the truck? Style? Model?"

Both Zeb and Noah shook their heads.

Sheriff Dablo took out a little pocket-sized notebook and started to write, speaking as he wrote.

"Three men, two Indians, one with a ponytail, and one white man wearing a cowboy hat. One Indian and one white man were beating up the second Indian male with a bat or stick. The body of the beaten man placed in back of an older, possibly brown, possibly dented truck. Make and model unknown. That sound about right to you boys?"

Noah and Zeb nodded. Everything sounded both scary and cool to Zeb.

Sheriff Dablo got on his two-way radio and called for Deputy Charlie Fritz. Zeb and Noah could hear his response.

"Roger that, Sheriff Dablo. I'll be there in ten minutes."

"Anything else you want to tell me, Zeb?"

"No. Nothing else that I can think of. Wait a second."

Once again Noah gave Zeb the death glare. This time the good angel on Zeb's shoulder did the talking.

"I thought I heard the man groan, once, maybe twice. Once on the ground and once when he was in the back of the truck. Yeah, I heard him groan twice."

"And you, Noah. Did Zeb forget anything?"

Noah rubbed his chin like he was thinking really hard. Zeb saw that he was acting like he did when he was about to tell a lie.

"I think they might have killed him," said Noah.

Zeb wondered why Noah was lying. Earlier Noah had said he was certain the man wasn't dead.

"What makes you say that?" asked Sheriff Dablo.

"Cause he didn't fight back. If he was alive, he would have fought back, unless he was a coward. He didn't even move at all when they lifted him up and tossed him into their truck."

"Maybe he was just mostly kind of unconscious," said Zeb, wishing for anything other than the worst possible outcome.

"Go home," said Sheriff Dablo. "Park your bikes in front of your house so I know you made it home. I'll drive by and check later. Got that?"

"Yes, sir," said Zeb.

"And don't leave your yard until morning. Got it?"

"Yes, sir," replied Zeb.

"If I catch you outside of your yard, I'll arrest the both of you and wake your parents up. Got that?"

"Yeah, I got it," added Noah dejectedly.

"I'll be by in the morning to have a little chat with your parents. They need to know what happened."

"Shit," said Noah.

"What was that?" asked Sheriff Dablo.

"My old man is gonna give us a real bad beatin' if you tell him we sneaked out and got caught around all this trouble."

Sheriff Dablo's eyes searched the boys for the truth. Zeb nodded, agreeing with his brother about the beating they might get. The sheriff believed them about the beating.

"If I knew who blew up the toilets and got them to help repair the building, out of the kindness of their hearts, maybe I could see that they were spared a thrashing they might actually having coming to them," said the sheriff.

"I blew up the ladies' bathroom."

The confession flew out of Zeb's mouth like lead pellets scattering from a shotgun blast. Noah stuffed his hands deep into his pockets. He stared at the ground, doing his best impression of an ignorant mute.

"Noah, any idea who blew up the men's toilet? Just so you know, I got a phone call that said two boys on almost identical Soaring Eagle Hiawatha bicycles were seen near the park toilets."

Tears fell from Noah's eyes. Zeb didn't understand his brother's reaction. He always acted like such a tough guy. Noah pushed the tip of his tennis shoe back and forth in the dirt for a long minute before quietly speaking up. When the words finally came out of his mouth, they were barely much more than a whisper.

"Okay. I blew it up. Now everybody's gonna know I ratted on myself. I'll never live it down."

"You two are going to volunteer, maybe even get a couple of your friends, let's say day after tomorrow at eight a.m. I'd bet if you do that, no one will ever know what happened except the three of us. Deal?"

Sheriff Dablo stuck out his hand. Zeb smiled, reached out, looked Sheriff Dablo in the eye and shook his hand as firmly as he could. The sheriff had great big hands. Reluctantly, Noah, without making eye contact, still staring into the dirt, weakly shook Sheriff Dablo's hand.

"Beat it," said Sheriff Dablo. "Beat if before Deputy Fritz sees you. His brother died in a German POW camp during the war. He's got a real soft spot in his heart for Ray Deyo. If he got wind that it was you two who blew up the biffies, well, he may not look too fondly upon it. Charlie doesn't act like it, but he's got a hell of a bad temper when somebody like Ray is getting picked on. Catch my drift?"

Zeb looked at Noah and could see fear in his eyes. He answered for the both of them.

"Yes, sir."

Noah and Zeb hopped on their bikes and sped wordlessly through the darkened streets of Safford until they reached the safety of home. The whooshing of tires on the still warm nighttime pavement and rutted dirt paths was the only sound save the hooting of a nearby owl perched in a dead pine tree.

2:03 A.M., JULY 4

"Hey, Sheriff. What's up?"

Sheriff Dablo shined his light on the pool of blood near his feet.

Deputy Charlie Fritz crouched near it, dabbed a finger at its edge and brought the finger to his nose.

"Any idea whose blood this is?" asked the deputy.

"Nope."

"How did you know it was here?"

"Anonymous tip," replied Sheriff Dablo.

"I called the office night clerk on the way over here. She said somebody, probably some kids, had been lighting off fireworks at the park."

"Yup."

"Think the two are related?" asked Charlie.

"How's that?" asked Sheriff Dablo.

Charlie was relatively new to the job. He was a good guy, a local guy, but not the sharpest knife in the drawer.

Charlie shined his light near the blood pool. He drew a circle with the beam on a specific spot.

"Just one second."

Deputy Fritz walked back to his vehicle and grabbed the official Graham County police camera. He took a half-dozen pictures. When he was done, he bent down and shined his flashlight on what looked like a short string.

"Yup."

"Yup, what?" asked Sheriff Dablo.

"That a fuse from an M-80. I'd recognize it anywhere. Maybe a kid blew their finger off," said Charlie. He followed a small trail of blood that ended short of the garbage bin.

"Have a look at this, Sheriff Dablo."

Jake walked behind the garbage bin. He spotted an abandoned bicycle.

"It's a Hiawatha. Pretty nice one. Somebody must have ditched it here. It's a good bike and it's certainly not garbage. Not even a rich kid throws away a bike this nice."

"When you're done here, put it in your vehicle and take it to the station. Somebody will probably come looking for it tomorrow," said Sheriff Dablo.

"Can do," replied Charlie.

"And call the hospital and see if anyone has come in tonight with bloody wounds."

Charlie nodded, walked a few feet away and made the call on his walkie-talkie. A moment later he approached Sheriff Dablo.

"I talked with Doc Yackley. I swear he must work twenty-four hours a day."

"What'd he have to say?" asked Jake.

"He said, and I quote, "Hell no.""

"Why don't you run over to the hospital and check it out anyway," said Jake. "I'll snoop around here some more."

"I'll be back when I'm done," said Charlie.

"No need for that. You've got a long day coming up, what with the parade, the fireworks and all. Call me if you find out anything that seems suspicious enough to be related to this blood."

Sheriff Dablo shined his flashlight on the blood.

"If not, call me anyway and let me know what you found out."

"Gotcha, Sheriff Dablo. Roger that."

Charlie walked around the area before heading to the hospital. He was certain he would find a kid with a missing finger or two getting stitched up by Doc Yackley.

Jake cordoned off the bloodstained area with some yellow police tape. The blood was mostly in a single area with another dozen or so medium and large sized drops creating a trail toward the middle of the alley. He gloved up and gathered some of the blood for evidence. He snooped around the area a little more and found a pair of boots near the dumpster. He examined them. They were worn, but definitely not trash. He eyed them closely, got out a rag, wiped them clean and proceeded to toss them in the dumpster. He jammed them underneath some other garbage. He took a final, quick trip around the large garbage bin. He found nothing related to the blood.

He was about to call it a night when two other things caught his eye. The first was a pencil. The leaded end had blood on it. The second object was in the middle of the blood pool. He shined a light on it. It was a human toe. A little toe. Upon finding the pencil he uttered a single word.

"Shit."

When he found the pencil, he cursed aloud.

"Goddamn it."

It didn't take him long to figure out what had happened.

As he placed the small toe in an evidence bag, he considered the amount of blood in the alley. It was a significant amount of blood to come from the loss of a little toe. Sheriff Dablo dropped the toe in a baggie. He broke the pencil in half and placed it in with the toe. He washed his hands with some cleaner he kept in the truck.

Glancing at his watch Sheriff Dablo realized it was still over three hours until sunrise. He needed to be the person to clear the scene of evidence. He couldn't do that until the sun rose. With that in mind he walked a half a block to an intersection that would be blocked off for the fourth of July parade. He grabbed two barriers and placed them so no one could accidentally disrupt the crime scene. He grabbed two more barriers and enlarged the cordoned off area, just in case. Next to the barriers were a dozen garbage cans meant to be used that day during the parade. Some had trash in them already. He reached into the baggie and grabbed the pencil halves. He placed one half in one garbage can and the other half in a separate garbage bin. Sheriff Dablo then placed the baggie with the toe in it on the ground. He brought his boot heel down hard on it several times. When he was done, the toe was unrecognizable as part of a human foot. He found a garbage can with trash in it and dumped the toe in it. He shredded the baggie and placed pieces of it in several other trash cans.

Charlie called him on the two-way radio.

"Sheriff Dablo, Deputy Charlie, over."

"What've you got, Charlie?"

Charlie said nothing, waiting for the proper protocol. Jake quickly figured out his deputy was doing everything by the book.

"Over. And, Charlie?"

"Yes, sir?"

"There's no need for protocol tonight. It's just you and me. Everyone else in town is still in bed."

"Probably not everyone, Sheriff Dablo. It's been a while since you worked the night shift. We got more than a few night creatures that like to roam Safford late at night or early in the morning."

"Right," said Sheriff Dablo. "What'd you find out?"

"I'm at the hospital. I talked with the admission nurse, Nurse Jerome. I also chatted for a minute with Doc Yackley. The only real business they've had tonight was a car accident with injuries, nothing serious, plus the usual kids with earaches and a couple of old people who thought they were having heart attacks. No one with wounds big enough to produce the amount of the blood we saw."

"You near Doc Yackley?" asked Jake.

"Yeah, he's right here."

"Let me talk with him."

Charlie handed the walkie-talkie handset to Doc.

"Jake."

"Doc."

"What's up?"

"Anyone come in tonight that lost a lot of blood?"

"Your memory getting' short?"

Before Jake could answer Doc carried on.

"Like I told Charlie earlier. Hell no."

"Will you call me if someone does? Come in with a significant amount of blood loss, that is."

"I can do that," replied Doc. "Are you looking for anything or anyone in particular?"

"Someone who might have lost a fair amount of blood. Possibly an adult Apache male."

"Anything else you want to know?"

"If someone does come in that has lost a lot of blood, I'd like to know who brought them in."

"Are you expecting that I'll see this person who lost blood soon?" asked Doc.

"Not really," replied Jake. "I suspect you won't see this person at all."

"Interesting hunch on your part."

Jake cleared his throat. He recognized what a careless statement he had just made.

"What I mean is that based on the amount of blood I found in the alley behind Klippel's, if someone was going to make a trip to the emergency room, they'd have done it right away."

"That means one of three things," said Doc.

"You're a detective as well as a doctor?" asked Jake.

"I watched every episode of *Columbo* three times," replied Doc.

"That makes you qualified enough to have a hunch," said Jake. "What are the three things?"

"One, he or she or it is already dead."

"Always a possibility," replied Jake. "But the amount of blood I found doesn't look like it was enough to cause death."

"Okay. Second possibility is that they took care of it themselves. I've seen people with an arm half cut off that tried to duct tape it back on."

"Yup. Could be. People do crazy things. And number three?"

"Somebody helped them out."

"I'll go with option three," said Jake.

"In that case you're looking for two people," said Doc.

"Thanks for your help, Doc."

"Glad to oblige."

7

9:00 A.M., JULY 4

Sheriff Dablo parked his truck in front of the Hanks' house. Through the kitchen window he could see Zeb and Noah's parents eating breakfast. He got out of his vehicle and walked to the door. He walked by a pair of Hiawatha Soaring Eagle bicycles lying on the ground. He peered past them and saw the pup tent Noah and Zeb had told him they were camping in. Jake knocked on the front door. Mrs. Hanks answered.

"Good morning, Sheriff Dablo."

Marta wiped her hands on her apron. Jake tipped his hat.

"Morning, Marta."

"What brings you over at this time of day?" she asked.

Before Jake could respond Jonas Hanks shouted from the breakfast nook.

"What'd the boys do now? Was it Noah? Or did both of 'em do something?"

"Nothing like that, Jonas," said Jake. "Someone reported seeing a couple of Hiawatha bicycles at the park. Deputy Fritz remembered your boys had Hiawatha Soaring Eagle bikes. I was just stopping by to see if they had been stolen."

"Take a look out back," shouted Jonas.

"Thanks, I will. Good day, Mrs. Hanks," said Jake, once again tipping his hat.

Slowly Marta shut the door, keeping her eye on the sheriff through the window as he walked toward the side of the house.

Sheriff Dablo shook the support pole of the canvas pup tent. He got no response. He pulled back the flap and saw the boys were still sound asleep.

"You two are going to miss the parade if you don't get going," said Jake.

Noah and Zeb opened their eyes.

"I thought you said we were good," said Noah.

"We are, but I need to go over what you saw last night again."

"Why? We told you everything we saw," said Noah.

"All the same, I need to go over things with you. Protocol."

"What things?" demanded Noah.

Sheriff Dablo heard the back door open. From the corner of his eye he spotted the boys' father coming toward the tent.

"I'll pick you up at eight tomorrow morning, so you can get to work on fixing up the park toilets. We'll talk then."

Sheriff Dablo pulled his head out of the tent.

"Problem, Sheriff Dablo?" asked Jonas Hanks.

"No, not that I know of."

"Cause if those little shits of mine are holding something from you, I'll whip it out of 'em with a willow stick."

"No, it's all good. No need for that. I do have one question for them," said Sheriff Dablo. "I need to know if they know of anyone else who has a bike like theirs."

"Noah, Zeb, get your asses out of those sleeping bags," barked Jonas Hanks. "Sheriff Dablo here has a question for you."

The boys scooted out of the tent, not wanting to risk a beating.

"Who else has a bike like the ones you boys ride?"

"I dunno," replied Noah.

"Eskadi Black Robes has one. He's in my class at school. His mom teaches at the high school. He goes to town school rather than the Rez school," said Zeb.

"Okay," said Sheriff Dablo.

Jonas Hanks, cup of coffee in hand, wandered toward his garage.

"Why do you want to know about the bike?" asked Zeb.

Noah, standing behind his younger brother, jabbed him in the ribs.

"There was one, just like yours. It was abandoned, leaning against the back of Klippel's dumpster. We found it last night," said Sheriff Dablo.

"Think hard. Does anyone else you know have a bike like that?"

"Maya Song Bird has a girl's version of the bike. But you know the crossbar is missing on a girl's bike. I suppose that makes it easier for them, so they don't have to lift their leg so high, like if they have a dress on or something."

"Thanks, Zeb. Noah, anything you can think of?" asked Sheriff Dablo.

"Nope. I got nothin' for ya'. Nothin' at all. I don't know anything."

Sheriff Dablo had a pretty good sense that Noah was lying.

"See you at eight sharp tomorrow morning," said Sheriff Dablo.

"What do we tell our dad?" whispered Zeb.

"Don't worry. I'll handle that."

Jake shut the flap on the tent, pivoted and bumped into the boys' father, who was making his return from the garage.

"Trouble?" asked Jonas.

"Quite the contrary. Both boys have volunteered to help clean up the city park tomorrow morning."

"Seriously? Zeb, I could see him doing that. But Noah? You sure he volunteered?"

"Yup. They volunteered. Both of them. Probably the free ice cream and hot dogs after the cleanup was the deciding factor," said Sheriff Dablo.

"Growing boys do pack it away. Glad you can get them to do something. They aren't much help around the house."

"Were you at that age?" asked Sheriff Dablo.

"Probably not. I'll admit that to you but not to those boys. I was kind of a good for nothing."

"I doubt I did much good for anyone at their age myself. I guess it goes with the age, the hormones and all that kind of crap."

"I suppose that's it."

"I'm picking them up at eight. I'll be a little early. Make sure they're ready."

The men shook hands. Jake headed for his truck. Jonas meandered to the middle of the backyard and stood, coffee cup in hand, staring toward Mount Graham. Zeb and Noah walked toward the house for breakfast.

"I'm getting' up early and skippin' out on cleaning up those toilets," said Noah. "Can you imagine what blown up poop does to the walls and everything?"

"We gotta go," said Zeb. "We said we would."

"You go then. Screw it. I got better things to do."

"But what about the sheriff wanting to talk to us some more?" asked Zeb.

"It was your Injun buddy, Eskadi Buffalo Robes…"

"Black Robes," interjected Zeb.

"Whatever. His bike was there. He probably was too. Let Sheriff Dablo figure it out. He's the cop. We're just kids."

"It's the fourth of July. We should be good citizens," said Zeb. "We should join the parade."

Noah shook his head.

"We're American kids. We should blow shit up. That's what we should do."

This time it was Zeb's turn to shake his head.

8

7:45 A.M., JULY 5

S heriff Dablo rolled up in front of the Hanks' house just as Noah was hopping on his bike. When Noah saw Sheriff Dablo, he cursed under his breath.

"I was just gonna ride down to the sheriff's office to meet you," said Noah.

"No need. I'm here now. Get your brother and let's get going. You can toss your bike into the back of my truck if you want."

"Nah," replied Noah, dumping his bike over.

Reluctantly, hands dug deeply into his pockets, Noah ambled through the back door of the family house, walked up to Zeb and smacked his brother on the back of the head.

"Your pal, the sheriff, is here for us."

Zeb rinsed out his cereal bowl, slipped on his tennis shoes and headed toward the sheriff's truck. Lollygagging behind was his brother.

"Let's go, boys. You've got work to do."

Sheriff Dablo headed toward the park. Ray Deyo and a couple of Boy Scouts were already at work cleaning up the mess and beginning to paint the inside and outside of the ladies' toilet building. Jake parked his vehicle. The boys opened their respective doors.

"Change of plans," announced Sheriff Dablo.

Noah let out a sigh of relief. He knew it was going to be over 110 degrees.

"Noah, you stay here and get to work with Mr. Deyo. He wants some help cleaning the blown-up toilets before the inside painting of the men's room begins."

Noah groaned loudly.

"Zeb stay in the car," said Sheriff Dablo.

"Where are you taking my brother?"

Noah was irate at the thought Zeb wasn't going to have to do any of the dirty work. Sheriff Dablo did not respond to Noah's question. He simply motioned Ray Deyo to the truck.

"This is Noah Hanks. He blew up the toilets. He wants to make it right."

Noah immediately protested.

"I didn't do it alone. Zeb did it too."

Zeb was only slightly shocked that his brother ratted him out.

"Is that right, Zeb?" asked Sheriff Dablo.

Zeb hung his head low.

"Yes, sir."

"Have Noah clean up his brother's part of the mess, too," said Sheriff Dablo. "Don't let him go home until the job is done."

Ray saluted the sheriff and grinned. Jake and Zeb headed down the road.

"Where we goin'?" asked Zeb.

Sheriff Dablo pointed his thumb toward the bed of his truck. Zeb turned and saw a Hiawatha bike just like his own, only the bike had red, white and blue tassels hanging from the holes of the handlebar grips and some old baseball cards held with clothespins in the spokes. It was the bike from the scene of the crime.

"Recognize the bike?"

"Yeah. It's Eskadi's bike, isn't it? It's the one you found in the alley by the blood, right?"

"That's good deductive reasoning. You are right. It is the bike from the alley that was leaning against Klippel's dumpster."

"We headed to the Rez?"

"I think Eskadi would like his bike back, don't you?"

"Sure, but..."

"But what?"

"It's evidence, isn't it?"

"I guess we'll know the answer to that after we talk with him," said Sheriff Dablo.

"I hope he's not in trouble," said Zeb. "He's my friend and he's a good guy. I know that it wasn't him that I saw behind Klippel's."

Zeb turned on the radio to KTKT, southern Arizona's favorite country and western station. It played a lot of oldies, along with the newer stuff. *Good Hearted Woman* by Waylon Jennings and Willie Nelson was playing. Sheriff Dablo hummed a bit then sang along. Zeb joined in.

"Like that song, young man?"

"I like Waylon and Willie," replied Zeb. "That's for sure."

"Me too. I think they've got long careers ahead of them."

Next up was *Cherokee Maiden* by Merle Haggard. Once again, they sang along. Zeb found himself wishing he had a dad like Sheriff Dablo. They pulled onto the Rez.

"You know where Eskadi lives?" asked Sheriff Dablo.

"Yes, sir. Just go up there and turn right. It's the yellow and red house on the left with the front porch that has a swing on it."

Eskadi was tossing a tennis ball against a cement wall as they drove into the dirt driveway. Sheriff Dablo and Zeb got out. Zeb ran over to his friend.

"Eskadi, you missing your bike?"

"Yeah. How'd you know that?" asked Eskadi.

"Come on. It's in the back of Sheriff Dablo's truck."

The boys ran to the truck where Sheriff Dablo had already removed the bicycle.

"This belong to you?"

"It does. Thanks for bringing it back. Where'd you find it?"

"It was in the back of Klippel's Flower store, by the dumpster," said Zeb.

"What was it doing there?" asked Eskadi.

"I was hoping you could tell me," said Sheriff Dablo.

"It was in the back of my dad's truck when Jimmy Song Bird borrowed it to pick up some stuff in town. He brought it back after I was in bed. When I got up in the morning, the bike wasn't in there. My dad said Song Bird didn't know what happened to it and offered to get me a new one. But my dad said we'd look around for it first. My dad figured some White boy stole it out of the truck when Jimmy Song Bird drove it to town."

"Is your dad around?" asked Sheriff Dablo.

Eskadi's father walked out of the house.

"Where'd you find the bike? I been lookin' all over hell for that thing."

"In town. Behind Klippel's."

Eskadi's dad nodded but said nothing.

"Good thing you found it. Eskadi's been having a bad couple of days."

"What happened?" asked Zeb.

"You know my dog, Einstein?"

"Yeah, he's a good dog," said Zeb.

"He *was* a good dog."

"Whaddaya mean?"

"Somebody shot him," said Eskadi.

"Who?" asked Zeb. "Why?"

"I don't know. All I know is Naiche Dreez threatened to shoot him a couple of times because he barked at night. Dreez is a scary guy. He might have done it. I don't know for sure, but I bet he did. He's both mean and ornery."

"That's the kind of guy who would shoot a dog," said Zeb.

"What do you think, Mr. Black Robes?" asked Sheriff Dablo.

Eskadi's dad shrugged his shoulders. Zeb noticed Eskadi's dad's knuckles were cut, like he had recently been in a fight.

"Where does this Dreez fella live?" asked Sheriff Dablo.

Eskadi's dad pointed across the way to a green house with a swing set in the front yard.

"Does Police Chief Baishan know about the threat?" asked Sheriff Dablo.

"Nope. Don't think it's something he'd want to get involved in."

"Why don't you boys play some ball. I'm going to go have a chat with Chief Baishan."

When Jake arrived at the tribal offices, Police Chief Kutli Baishan was sitting with his boots propped up on his desk. He stood and gave Jake's hand a firm grip.

"Jake, what brings you up my way?" asked Chief Kutli Baishan.

"Kutli, good to see you."

Kutli was relatively new to his job. Jake had only a few interactions with him and wasn't certain how he would react when asked a favor.

"Professional visit?" asked Kutli.

"Yes. One of your people and one of my people were seen beating up an Indian in the alley behind Klippel's the night before last. We found a bicycle that belongs to Eskadi Black Robes leaning against the dumpster near where the fight was. The whole thing left a lot of blood."

"You don't think Eskadi is involved do you? He's hardly a troublemaker."

"No. We've got a description of the men, but Naiche Dreez threatened to kill his dog, and the dog was found shot dead. Eskadi's dad's hands look like he's just been in a fight. It's probably unrelated, but I thought you should know. Just so you know, Naiche got into a fight at Windy's Bar in town last night. He was looking for trouble."

"Who with?"

"Some local drunk. One of those pointless, stupid fights that only drunks get into."

"Did he win or lose?" asked Kutli.

"Both of them took a lot of punches," said Jake. "From what I heard it was a toss-up. In the end both of them just plain ran out of gas."

"Dake Black Robes is a peaceable fellow. I doubt he would beat up on Naiche even though Naiche is a real drunken, good-for-nothing, pain in the ass who has threatened his family."

"You know about that? I mean Naiche threatening to kill Eskadi's dog?"

"Who doesn't? Naiche is always shooting his mouth off."

"Let's go talk to Naiche," suggested Jake. "It's early. He's probably sober or hung over."

Chief Baishan glanced at his watch. It was twenty minutes of nine.

"Yeah, pretty good chance he's still sober. I don't know if he drinks for breakfast. He might. Let's take my vehicle," said Chief Baishan. "If he was involved in something in town and sees your truck, he's likely to run or take a pot shot at you."

The men drove slowly through the Rez streets to Naiche's house. They knocked on the door. Eventually, he responded. When he finally did come to the door, it was obvious he was hung over and had recently been on the losing end of a fight. He also had a piece of a dirty cotton ball sticking out of his left ear.

"Naiche," said Chief Baishan. "This is Sheriff Dablo."

"I know who he is," grunted Naiche, staring Jake in the eyes.

Jake extended a hand. Naiche didn't move a muscle. Jake pulled his hand back and away from the rotund but rough looking Indian who wore his shiny, black hair to his shoulders.

"What happened to you?" asked Chief Baishan.

"What do you mean?" asked Naiche.

"You look like somebody who just got their ass kicked. That's what."

"I took a tumble the other night. I was drunk."

"Where did that happen?"

"Early Chatto's place. He'll tell ya."

"Jake tells me you got drunk at Windy's the other night," said Chief Baishan.

"Don't remember nothin' like that," replied Naiche.

"You're standing kind of crooked. Hurt your back?" asked Chief Baishan.

"Sore foot," replied Naiche.

"You shoot any dogs lately?" asked Chief Baishan, getting right to the point.

"Hell no. I love dogs. I'd never shoot a dog. Except one that was rabid."

"Okay," said Chief Baishan. "Better get those cuts on your face looked at. Your nose looks broken too."

Naiche wiggled his nose between his thumb and first finger before shutting the door. Jake and Kutli walked slowly to Kutli's truck.

"You say Eskadi's dad's knuckles look like he's been in a fight?"

"Yes. I did. But he's a bare-knuckled boxer on the side."

"What?" asked Jake.

"It's a Rez thing. A guy can make a thousand bucks, cash, on a good night. It's illegal, but to be honest the department has a long history of looking the other way when it comes to that matter."

"Makes sense his meat hooks look the way they do."

"His mitts are always beat up."

Jake nodded. He had not heard about the bare-knuckled boxing, but it seemed like a Rez thing. He let it go.

"Here's what happened," said Chief Baishan. "Naiche shot Eskadi's dog. Eskadi's dad, Dake, was pissed off. I know him pretty well. He's a turn the other cheek kind of Christian man. He likely went to Medicine Man Jimmy Song Bird and prayed with him for guidance. The word about the dog killing got around and some Apache and a white guy beat the hell out of Naiche. Somehow or other Eskadi's bike got left behind at Klippel's. I'd bet whoever beat the hell out of Naiche borrowed Dake's truck and Eskadi's bike was in the back. I guess there wasn't room for both Naiche and the bike in the back of Dake's truck. That makes sense because it's a short bed truck and always full of junk. Seems like they took out the bike, leaned it against the dumpster and threw Naiche in the back of the truck. They drove Naiche back to the Rez and dropped him off. They didn't want the beating to be connected with town. Naiche took his beating. The dog is dead. Eskadi has his bike back and there's a hundred stray dogs around. He's a smart kid, he'll pick a smart dog and train it up good. End of story."

"Sounds reasonable enough," said Jake. "Can you explain the cotton ball in his ear?"

"Whoever beat him up probably jammed a pencil in his ear to rupture his ear drum," said Chief Baishan.

"Why?"

"It's an Apache way of sending a message."

Jake gave him a confused look.

"I've lived here all my life. That's how shit goes down."

"You gonna do anything about it?" asked Jake.

"What's to do? The dog is dead. Eskadi's bike is back. An ounce of flesh has been extracted from Naiche. What more is there to do?"

Jake nodded. In his mind a little frontier justice had its place. It seemed as fair as the court system the Rez used. Song Bird, no doubt, would be glad to hear that Chief Baishan was not going to spend any time looking into the beating Naiche Dreez had taken. The secret of who gave the beating would remain confidential. Jake breathed a little easier.

9

10 A.M., JULY 5

FRIENDS AND FISHING

T he two lawmen drove back to the tribal police chief's office. Jake thanked Kutli for his help. Jake was more than a little grateful that the tribal police chief understood true justice. No doubt it would make things easier and prevent potential trouble for the cowboy and his Indian friend that had done the deed.

"I've got another favor to ask," said Jake.

"You're going to owe me a couple by the time this is over."

"I am," replied Jake.

"What can I do for you?"

"Is there any chance you're driving into Safford tonight?"

"I am."

"When?"

"Around supper time. Probably at six or seven."

"Could you drive Zeb Hanks back to town and drop him off at my office?"

"Not a problem."

"Thanks. He'll be at Eskadi's. I'm going to drop them both off at Song Bird's with some fishing gear."

"Summer time, boys and fishing. Can't beat that."

"You got that right."

"I'll bet you long for those days as much as I do."

"I do," replied Kutli.

"Thanks. I owe you at least one, maybe two favors."

Kutli smiled. He enjoyed having the upper hand.

Jake drove to Eskadi's house. Zeb and Eskadi were horsing around, roughhousing and joking like adolescent boys so easily do.

"Hey."

Eskadi and Zeb were startled by Jake. From the tone of the sheriff's voice they assumed they were in trouble.

"Do you two want to go bass fishing in the reeds along the east edge of the San Carlos Lake?" asked Jake.

Zeb frowned painfully.

"I don't have my fishing gear."

"I'll have to borrow some," said Eskadi. "I can probably find some for you too."

"I brought enough for the both of you. Just make sure you're back here by six. Chief Baishan is going to give Zeb a ride back to town."

"Great," said Eskadi. "I'll tell my mom. Maybe she'll make us some peanut butter and jelly sandwiches to take along."

"I gotcha covered. There's a cooler full of sandwiches and soda pop," said Sheriff Dablo.

Ten minutes later they arrived at Medicine Man Jimmy Song Bird's house. He was sitting out front with two young girls. One of them got up immediately upon seeing the sheriff's truck. She ran toward it. A long-drawn look of disappointment spread across her lips.

"Da-ad. What are you doing here? I thought you said I could hang out all day with Maya."

Jenny Dablo's long hair fell to her waist. At eleven years of age she was already an innocent, blossoming beauty. Her friend, Maya Song Bird, was just as pretty. Maybe even more so.

"I've got some business with Song Bird."

Maya ran joyfully to the truck. The girls peeked inside and giggled when they saw Eskadi and Zeb.

"I've got to drop these boys off. They want to do some fishing. Bass fishing."

"That's my favorite," said Jenny.

"Mine too," added an excited Maya.

"Hey, isn't that my gear in the back of your truck," said Jenny.

Jake looked over his shoulder toward the truck bed.

"By gosh and by golly, I guess it is. Maybe the boys will take you fishing with them?"

The inquiry was less of a question than it was a hint. The girls nodded joyfully at each other. As beautiful as these young girls were, they were both wild tomboys.

"You boys okay taking Maya and Jenny fishing with you? As a favor to me?"

Eskadi, the bolder of the two boys, turned to Zeb as he spoke.

"I've fished with Maya before. She knows her stuff. We'll catch enough fish for three or four dinners. Plus, it's Jenny's gear."

"Okay," said Zeb. "It's fine with me."

"Maya, get your gear. Boys, please behave like gentlemen. Let the girls sit in the cab. You two can hop in the back of the truck. I'll give you a ride over there. You'll have to walk back."

Maya grabbed some gear from Song Bird and all four kids hopped in the back of the sheriff's truck. Ten minutes later they all had their poles in the water.

Sheriff Dablo headed back to Song Bird's.

It didn't take long for the four teenagers to turn fishing talk into what had happened in the alley a few nights earlier, and, of course, the blowing up of the toilets at the park.

"Zeb Hanks, you did what?" said Maya. "I always thought you were such a goody-two-shoes."

"My brother made me do it," replied Zeb.

"Every young person must watch out for peer pressure," said Jenny.

They all laughed. A recent symposium at school had taught them about peer pressure and why to avoid it.

"Are you ever going to have a boyfriend, Maya?" asked Eskadi.

"She likes Zeb," interjected Jenny.

Zeb's face turned the color of a freshly picked beet. Everyone laughed.

"What are you gonna be when you get older?" asked Jenny.

"I'm going to college. Then, I'm going to be a professor," said Eskadi. "Later on, I'm going to be a politician and become president. When I'm president, I'm going to enforce all the old Indian treaties."

"You are a dreamer," said Maya. "My dad says that won't happen for a thousand years."

"How does he know that?" asked Zeb.

"Do you know my father?" asked Maya.

"Some. Only a little. I know he is a respected medicine man in your tribe," replied Zeb.

Maya chuckled. So did Eskadi.

"Song Bird is known by all the tribes. He knows the tribes. He knows the heavens. It is said he has been blessed by many gods. Even the Creator of all things has blessed Song Bird," added Eskadi.

With Eskadi's words a quiet reverence passed among the adolescents. Zeb was confused about how they all knew that.

"What's the story about what's going to happen in a thousand years?" asked Zeb.

"My father, from his relationship with other medicine men, especially the Ute and Ojibway medicine men, knows future history."

"What?" asked Zeb incredulously.

"Stuff that's going to happen in the future."

"How can that be?" asked Zeb.

"I don't expect a White boy from town to believe or even understand for that matter,.but I'll tell you anyway. There is a place in southwestern Colorado and another in northern New Mexico where a sleeping giant lives. The giants are resting in mountains. In fact, the mountaintop forms a sleeping Indian warrior. The warrior in New Mexico is facing Ute Mountain on the Ute Reservation. The Utes say the mountain is a grand warrior resting from battling against great evil."

"Great evil? Do you mean the devil?" asked Zeb.

"Not the devil that you think of," said Eskadi. "Not the one with a pitchfork and a pointed tail."

Everyone laughed except Zeb. He didn't know what they meant.

"That great evil was the invasion of the White men, the brown men, the black men and others who were not First People."

"The First People?" asked Zeb. "Do you mean Adam and Eve?"

Eskadi and Maya chuckled knowingly. Jenny followed their lead.

"When the sleeping giant rises up in a thousand years, all of the Indian nations will band together and retake the land that is rightfully theirs," explained Maya.

"To make sure that happens, every year a three-day Sun Dance is held on a sagebrush flat over the giant Sleeping Ute's heart. It keeps his heart alive. It keeps the memory of a living truth for the First People full of hope," added Eskadi.

"There are sleeping giant Indians almost everywhere," said Maya.

"Yes, yes," chimed in Eskadi, willing and excited to share his knowledge. "They are in Montana, Wyoming, Hawaii and even Canada. The sleeping giant in Canada is called Nanabijou. It is seven miles long."

Zeb was stunned, mostly because what his friends were saying rang true to his heart. A great quiet followed the excited talk. The youngsters all seemed to lapse into a state of deep thought. The restlessness and excitement of young people together became an ancient calmness. Eskadi broke the silence.

"We'll see what happens," he said. "For now, we must live in the present. I heard Song Bird say that nothing lasts, but everything is eternal."

Zeb's head was spinning. He felt ignorant and confused, yet somehow it all made a kind of sense that only the innocent can understand. Eskadi picked up a handful of dust. He stood and slowly allowed the dust to drop from his hand. The four teenagers watched as the dust faded and dissipated. The mood, as quickly as it had changed, returned to normal.

"What are you going to become Jenny?"

"I'm going to move to Phoenix and become the weather lady on TV," said Jenny.

"I'm going to Hollywood and become a movie star," added Maya.

"What about you, Zeb?" asked Eskadi.

"I like Sheriff Dablo. I think he's about the nicest guy I've ever met. Maybe I'll become Sheriff of Graham County one day."

A small mouth bass took a hard bite out of Zeb's bait and began working his line. Everyone watched closely as the fish put up a darn good fight. Much to everyone's delight and among many oohs, aahs and laughter, he reeled it in. Unspoken precious moments quickly created deep friendships.

"This is just perfect," said Maya.

"It would have been more perfect if I had caught the fish," said Eskadi.

They all laughed.

"At times like this it feels like we've known each other forever," said Maya.

Zeb, Maya, Jenny and Eskadi looked at one another. None of them had any words for what they were so intensely feeling. Yet, no one felt the least bit awkward.

Eskadi had one final word before they headed back.

"I wish today would never end."

The easy silence that followed told them all it was a universal feeling they shared.

Little could Zeb know what today really marked the beginning of. Nor could he possibly imagine how the rest of his life would be affected by the relationships that were quickly developing.

10

1 WEEK LATER

IN THE BEGINNING

Sheriff Dablo pulled his truck in front of the Hanks' home. When he rang the doorbell, Marta glanced through the small vertical window before opening the front door. Jake politely removed his hat and held it in his hand at his side. The sheriff got right to his point.

"Marta, I have a favor to ask of you."

"Yes?"

"Would you mind if Zeb spends a day fishing and a night camping with me and the San Carlos medicine man out on the Rez?"

"Certainly not. It's good for a boy to have positive role models. What's up?"

"Do you know Jimmy Song Bird, the medicine man out at the San Carlos?"

"Only by reputation. I've heard rumors that besides being wise and a great healer that he has done traditional Apache healing medicine for some of the Beatles and some of the Rolling Stones. Is that true?"

"It is. How did you know about that? Song Bird sort of keeps that information close to the vest."

"Helen and I were having tea and blueberry muffins one day..."

"She loves her blueberry muffins," interjected Jake. "And she knows everything that goes on in Graham County."

"She most certainly does. Well, just as she bit into her blueberry muffin a song by Paul McCartney came on the radio. The song was *Band On The Run*. We were in a funny mood and we ended up calling it *Bands Got the Runs*. Silly girl talk. We got to talking about how Paul owns some land and a house about an hour from here. Somewhere over by Tucson is what we heard."

"I know exactly where it is if you ever want to drive by. I'd be glad to give you the tour," said Jake.

"Someday, maybe."

"Keep it in mind."

"Anyway, Helen said she'd heard that Song Bird had done some healing work for Paul and his wife. She also knew that the Rolling Stones used to rent that big mansion out in Eden, just north of Safford. She'd also heard Song Bird had worked with them."

"It's all true," said Jake. "I don't know the details, but I know it happened. So, it's okay to take Zeb on an overnight?"

"I don't know what Jonas would think of it, but I'm sure he won't mind since Zeb is going with you, Jake. I don't know what he thinks of Song Bird, or if he even knows who he is. He doesn't care for Indians in general," replied Marta. "When were you thinking of taking him camping?"

"Tonight, if that works," replied Jake. "Sorry I didn't give you more warning, but it came up sort of at the last minute. Song Bird and I do this at least once a month. Last time out, I was telling him I thought Zeb was a good kid that could learn some things from him. Zeb's met Song Bird a few times, but they don't really know each other."

"I'm sure he'll want to go. I've heard him talking a lot about fishing with Jenny and Maya. Are they going along?"

"No, this is a boys only trip."

"What time do you want to pick him up?"

Jake glanced at his watch.

"Six? Is that okay?"

"Should I feed him?"

"No, Song Bird has a special stew he makes for these things," chuckled Jake.

"What's in it?"

"You don't want to know."

Marta broke into spontaneous laughter. It was the first time she had laughed in months.

J ake picked up Zeb promptly at six. He wanted to expose the young man not only to how another culture lived, a subject he was fairly new too as well, but he and Jimmy Song Bird wanted to let him in on a hobby that could educate him.

"How come the medicine man wants to see me? I met him that day I went fishing with Maya, Jenny and Eskadi," asked Zeb. "I said hello to him a couple of other times. I don't really know him that good."

"Maybe he wants to make sure you're nice to his daughter," replied Jake.

Zeb blushed. He had a crush on Maya Song Bird, but he had never told anyone.

"Aw, c'mon," said Zeb. "Why am I really here? Am I in trouble?"

"He wants to teach you about the stars in the sky. He and I have been studying them for a few years now. I told him I thought you would like to learn about them too."

"Cool," replied Zeb.

Jake drove to a remote part of the reservation. By the time they arrived both he and Zeb were hungry. They spotted Song Bird leaning over a cook pot. The medicine man looked old to Zeb, but, then again, all men over thirty years of age looked old to him. Such is the eye of youth.

The aroma wafted through the open windows of Jake's truck.

"Man, that smells good," said Zeb. "Do you know what it is?"

"Road kill stew."

Zeb couldn't tell if Jake was joking or not.

"Really?"

"Yup."

A sour look overcame Zeb's face.

"I promise you that you will love it," said Jake.

"Really?"

"Yup."

Song Bird, with his back to them, motioned them toward the fire and cookpot.

"Hungry?" asked Song Bird.

"I guess," replied Zeb, staring into the stewpot.

"When I was your age, I was hungry all the time."

A strange feeling came over Zeb. He couldn't tell if it was from the exotic aromas coming from the stewpot or something else. In any case he swooned.

"Are you feeling okay, young man?" asked Song Bird.

"I'm fine. It's just I've never had..."

"Road kill stew?"

"Yeah," replied Zeb. "Road kill stew. It sounds kind of weird."

"You're lucky. It's all deer, rabbits and squirrel. No skunks. No mice."

Zeb gulped loudly enough for the men to hear. Song Bird laughed so hard he cried. Jake held his sides as he laughed heartily. Zeb realized he was being initiated into a very private club. The meal was just the beginning. The stew had an amazing taste. It was one Zeb would never forget as long as he lived.

The men had eaten quietly, barely speaking. Zeb was used to meal time consisting of his father's rants and raves and a general sense of unease. After they were done eating and the dishes were cleaned, Song Bird pulled a flask seemingly from out of thin air and poured a yellow-green greasy looking liquid into three small glasses. Song Bird handed one to Jake, one to Zeb and kept one for himself.

"To a boy who is about to become a man," said Song Bird. "To learning some of the secrets of the heavens above and what they mean."

"Hear, hear," replied Jake.

Zeb smiled curiously. He was intrigued, but he didn't know why or about what. These men obviously had something in mind for him. He had absolutely no idea what exactly that was. An hour later, after many curious toasts that Zeb would later learn to be lessons in the rights of passage that led from youth to manhood, Song Bird became quiet. Jake followed his lead. Zeb watched as the men seemed to be praying. After a short time, when the day began to darken into night, Song Bird rose to his feet.

"Follow me," he said.

Jake and Zeb followed the medicine man down a path into a small box canyon. Between the stone walls it was darker than any nighttime Zeb had ever imagined.

"Here is where you learn," said Song Bird. "This is a sacred place."

Jake built a small fire. The blue, orange and yellow flames provided an extraordinary amount of light in the extreme darkness. The blackness of night became almost like the light of day as the flames from the small fire danced shadowy figures on the canyon walls. Song Bird remained silent. Zeb stood frozen. When the fire was glowing brightly, Zeb spotted a platform with a handmade totem sitting atop it.

"Young man, what do you need to learn first?" asked Song Bird.

Zeb was confounded. He had no idea what the old medicine man was speaking about. He had no idea how to answer the simple question.

"I, I don't even know what to say," replied Zeb.

"That's good. Then let's start at the beginning."

"Beginning of what?" asked Zeb.

"The beginning of everything," replied Song Bird. "The foundation of all that will ever be."

Jake, receiving some cue from Song Bird, covered the fire with a blanket. Strangely, the blanket did not burn.

"In the beginning," explained Song Bird. "There was only darkness. Suddenly a small bearded man appeared. He is called the One Who Lives Above."

"God?" asked Zeb.

"The Creator," replied Song Bird. "But you may call Him God if that is what is comfortable for you."

"Okay," replied Zeb, scratching his head as if that might make him understand more clearly.

"The One Who Lives Above appeared. He rubbed his eyes as if he had just awakened. The Creator then rubbed his hands together. All at once a little girl appeared. She was called the Girl-Without-Parents. The creator rubbed his face with his hands and instantly there stood the Sun-God. Again, Creator rubbed his sweaty brow and from his hands dropped another god. This one was called Small-Boy. Now there were four gods. Then he created Tarantula, Big Dipper, Wind, Lightning-Maker and Lightning-Rumbler. All four gods shook hands so that their sweat mixed together."

Zeb's head was spinning. His face was covered in beads of perspiration. Song Bird reached over and rubbed an ancient, warm hand against Zeb's forehead. He showed his dampened hand to Zeb and Jake.

"The sweat of the gods is with us."

Zeb could barely follow Song Bird's story, much less grab its meaning. He had lived his youth learning from the Latter-Day Saints that Jesus Christ, acting under the direction of God the Father, created this and other worlds to make possible the immortality and eternal life of human beings who already existed as spirit children of the Father. He had also learned from his friends who attended other churches that their belief was that God had created the world in seven days. He had little reason to doubt either the Book of Mormon or the biblical versions. But here, in this mystical setting, his views of the beginning of all things were shifting. As Song Bird continued, Zeb felt himself being pulled into another type of world.

"Then Creator rubbed his palms together. A small, round, brown ball fell from his hands. All those present took turns kicking it. Each time they kicked the ball it grew larger and larger. Creator told Wind to go inside the ball and blow it up. Then Tarantula spun a black cord. He attached it to the ball and went to the east, pulling as hard as he could. He repeated this exercise with a blue cord to the south, a yellow cord to the west and a white cord to the north."

Jake leaned in and whispered to Zeb.

"The four directions are very important to know about if you want to understand Indian culture."

Zeb nodded. He wanted to understand. But everything was so new and different that he felt as lost as a sailor in a fog bank. Song Bird must have sensed Zeb's confusion. He turned to him and spoke.

"Creation was not a simple process. How could it have been?"

Once again, Zeb nodded as Song Bird held his arms overhead indicating that Zeb should behold the universe. For the first time in his life Zeb actually gave Creation more than just a passing thought.

"When he was done, the brown ball had become the earth. The Creator once again rubbed his hands together. This time Humming-bird appeared. Creator told Hummingbird, 'Fly all over the earth. Tell us what you see.' When Hummingbird returned, he reported that there was water on the west side. He told Creator, 'The earth rolls and bounces.' The Creator listened closely to Hummingbird. The Creator thought and thought. Then he made four giant posts. One was black, one blue, one yellow and one was white. The Creator then commanded the Wind to place the giant posts at the four cardinal points of the earth. When the wind had done this, the earth became still," explained Song Bird.

Everything around Zeb seemed to have become still, just like in Song Bird's story. He could hear the wind rustle in the trees, the water running through the canyon, animals sneaking through the night and what Song Bird would later call the breath of the universe. Almost as an afterthought Song Bird spoke once again.

"The creation of the people, animals, birds, trees and everything of that nature takes place after that."

Song Bird glanced at Zeb and sensed his confusion.

"But I think that is enough for the moment. Zeb, I want you to think about this. When you have questions, bring them to me," said Song Bird.

"Okay, but right now I don't even know what to ask," said Zeb. "I don't even know where to begin."

"You will," replied Song Bird. "It may be in the distant future, but the questions and many of the answers will come in the form of an Echo."

Song Bird then made an eerily beautiful trilling sound that echoed down the canyon, seemingly to infinity. Zeb intuitively knew this was not the Echo that Song Bird was speaking about.

Zeb shook his head. His was more bewildered than ever. Song Bird and Jake began to harmonize in a peaceful chant. The rhythm was simple. With a nod of his head, Song Bird encouraged Zeb to join them. Joining the men in the song was as simple as breathing. Time became irrelevant. Later, when something changed, Zeb didn't know what, Jake tapped him between the shoulder blades. Zeb assumed he had somehow fallen asleep.

"Sorry, I didn't even know I nodded off," said Zeb.

"You didn't sleep," said Song Bird. "You dreamt yourself into another place and time. Your lessons have begun."

11

LATER THAT NIGHT

AWAKE FROM THE DREAM

Jake shined the beam of a laser flashlight to the center of the canyon. Roughly fifty feet in front of them was the largest telescope Zeb had ever seen.

"Wow. Cool."

"It's more than cool," said Jake. "It can give you a peek into a world that the naked eye can never see."

"Where'd you get it? I've got a little one. I've never seen anything like that, even in books," said Zeb.

"One of the scientists on Mount Graham gave it to me as a gift. It's a long story. I helped him out of a jam, I guess. He was grateful. Song Bird and I have been using it for three years now."

"Where should we begin with young Zebulon Hanks?" asked Song Bird.

"Let's start with something every boy knows, the Big Dipper."

"There it is," shouted Zeb with powerful enthusiasm.

"Have a look through the telescope," said Jake. "Tell us what you see."

Zeb pointed the telescope toward the Big Dipper. He studied carefully.

"It's a dipper, a big one."

Jake and Song Bird chuckled and felt their own enthusiasm rising.

"It has four stars in its bowl and three more on its handle. Seven stars in the Big Dipper. I've looked at it a hundred times and never thought about counting the number of stars in it," said Song Bird.

"Now look at the bowl and draw an imaginary line between the two stars that form the top of the bowl and follow it outward until you see a bright star," said Jake.

"I see it, I see it."

"That is the North Star. Men in ships for thousands of years have used it for navigational purposes. We live in the desert, but we Indians have used it for thousands upon thousands of years to give us direction," said Song Bird.

"The North Star is also called Polaris," said Jake. "It lies in a direct line with the axis of the earth. Because of that, it appears to never move."

Zeb stared at the constellation.

"Song Bird," Zeb asked. "How was the Big Dipper made? Did the Creator make it?"

"You ask a good question. There is a story behind the creation of the Big Dipper. It is a tale of wolves, coyotes and bears."

"Please tell me the story," pleaded Zeb.

"Of course. That is why you are here, to learn. The story goes like this. Once there were five wolves who would share meat with Coyote. One night the wolves were staring at the sky. Coyote asked the wolves what they were looking at. The wolves said there were two animals up in the sky, and they wanted to get to them but couldn't. Coyote grinned slyly and offered them what he called an easy way to reach them."

"What was it?" asked Zeb.

"Coyote then took his bow and shot an arrow into the sky where it stuck. He shot another arrow which stuck into the first arrow. Then he shot another and another until the chain of arrows reached the ground. The five wolves and Coyote climbed the arrows into the sky. The oldest wolf took his dog along. When they reached the sky, the wolves could see that the animals were grizzly bears. The wolves went near the bears. They sat there looking at the bears. The bears looked back at the wolves. Coyote thought the wolves and the bears looked good sitting there. So, he left them and removed his arrow ladder. The three stars of the handle of the Big Dipper and the two stars of the bowl near the handle are the wolves. The two stars on the front of the bowl are the bears. The tiny star by the wolf in the middle of the handle is the dog," explained Song Bird.

Zeb listened intensely to the tale Song Bird offered. It was complicated and had many parts. He gave it a long thought before saying anything.

"I understand," said Zeb.

The medicine man could readily see that Zeb would be a worthy student.

"I think we should give you an Apache name," said Song Bird.

The mere idea of having another name, an Apache name, confused and excited Zeb.

"Me? An Apache name?"

"Zeb, I guess I should ask you first. Would you like an Apache name?"

"I've never really thought about it too much. But I have wondered what my name would be if I was an Indian. Yes, I'd like an Apache name."

Jake and Song Bird built a new fire.

"Zeb, go stand behind the fire," said Song Bird.

Song Bird and Jake silently stared at Zeb. They could see him clearly in the near darkness as the flames flickered and ashes flew upward.

"Zeb seems to disappear in the darkness then return," said Jake.

"His skin is white, but not like the White man. His skin is white like that of a ghost," said Song Bird.

"And his hair is black as midnight," added Jake.

"We shall call him it'een góshé hu iz naki ti tł'é'gona'áí dii dałaá," said Song Bird.

"What does it mean?" asked Zeb.

"The Little Sheriff Who is Both Night and Day," said Song Bird.

A surge of pride welled up inside of Zeb. For the first time in his life, he felt like more than just a boy. He had a vague sense that he was becoming a man.

The beginning of Zeb's education by Jake and Song Bird had been birthed again. The lessons would go on until none of them walked the earth any longer. But first his life would change dramatically.

Song Bird and Jake talked deep into the night. Zeb laid atop his sleeping bag watching the stars until he drifted off to sleep. Then something, perhaps it was the lowering of the tones of the men doing the conversing, woke him. He laid as still as was humanly possible and arced his ears toward the men's conversation. Could he be hearing them correctly? He didn't want to believe his ears.

"You're sure Chief Kutli won't be a problem?" asked Jake.

"I'm certain. Naiche Dreez is nothing but trouble. If Kutli had been with us, he would have helped," replied Song Bird. "He'll never even open an investigation into Naiche's beating, even if Naiche files a complaint. The laws are a little looser on the Rez when it comes to that sort of thing."

Zeb heard every word. What *sort of thing* were they talking about?

Zeb turned his head to see the silhouettes of Medicine Man Jimmy Song Bird and Sheriff Jake Dablo. He blinked and did a double take. The image of the sheriff's cowboy hat matched exactly what he had seen that night behind Klippel's store. When Song Bird turned to say something to Jake, his ponytail matched precisely what Zeb had seen that night as well. Could it be that Song Bird and Jake had beaten Naiche with a baseball bat? No, it couldn't be. They weren't those kind of men. Now, wider awake than ever, Zeb tuned into their conversation.

"What was with cutting off his little toe and jamming a pencil in his ear?" asked Jake.

"The pencil punctured his eardrum. It will heal up for the most part. But he will have enough hearing loss so that he will be concerned about people sneaking up on him. That will make him less likely to sneak around and do bad things. It's a little pain and a big lesson."

"Got it," replied Jake. "Sort of like breaking a couple of fingers on someone's punching hand so they can't hit as hard."

"Right. Just enough to slow someone down so they think about what they are doing," added Song Bird.

"And cutting off his little toe?" asked Jake.

"Old time tradition. He can still walk, but he can't run away as fast. If he tries any of his bullshit, he'll get caught because he'll be a step or two slower. Plus, it's a good reminder that each time he walks the earth that he has done wrong."

"I wish there was a better way," said Jake. "I don't feel bad about what we did, but I don't feel all that good about it."

"White man's guilt," said Song Bird. "It's your burden to carry. An Indian feels guilty about other things."

"Like what?"

"You'd know if you were an Indian," said Song Bird.

"Did you know the pencil you used and toe you cut off fell out of your pocket? Luckily, I found them and disposed of the evidence."

"That's what makes you a good sheriff," said Song Bird.

The men both lit cigarettes and sat quietly. The sounds of the desert night filled Zeb's ears. He leaned forward to hear anything the men might say. Finally, Song Bird spoke.

"Sometimes we have to do the wrong things, but for the right reasons."

Jake grunted in agreement. The men pulled their blankets closer to the fire and within a minute both were snoring. Zeb watched the stars move across the sky.

Could a man do the wrong thing for the right reason? Was that even possible? Zeb fell into a deep sleep, deeper than any sleep he had ever experienced. He dreamed of a man, a man that looked to be from a time in a book Zeb had read about fables. The man was handsome and well dressed. He looked to be very wealthy. He was surrounded by beautiful women, platters full of food and cups full of drinks. The man was sweating like it was a hot summer day in the desert. But, by the way the beautiful women and other men in the dream looked, it was just an ordinary day. Then, in his dream, Zeb saw the man looking up. Over his head was a sword, a razor-sharp sword. It was held precariously by a single thread. Zeb looked back at the man and saw his own face on the body of a grown-up man. Still in the dream, Zeb looked at everything around him before getting up and walking away. He looked back and saw the sword turn into a dove and fly away. An old, wise looking man spoke to him.

"Sometimes it is hard to know what to do and sometimes it isn't. You will know what to do when the time comes."

He woke with a start. He must have shouted something in his sleep as in the next moment Song Bird and Jake were standing over him.

"You okay?" asked Jake.

Zeb shook his head. He was not okay. But he could say nothing.

Song Bird knelt next to Zeb and placed his hands on his shoulders.

"Were you dreaming?

Zeb nodded that he had been.

"What about?"

Zeb could not control his tongue. Words uncontrollably came bursting from his mouth.

"Can I do a bad thing if it is for a good reason?"

"The world is a strange and beautiful place," replied Song Bird. "Your question is a good one, but a complicated one."

"Did you overhear us talking?" asked Jake.

Zeb could not lie to the men who were ushering him into manhood.

"Yes."

"Then I think you know the answer," replied Jake.

"Go back to sleep, it'een góshé hu iz naki ti tł'é'gona'áí dii dałaá.

Your dreams will always guide you. Have faith in understanding what is unknowable. Believe in your heart."

Zeb laid his head down and drifted off into a sea of dreams. His life, it seemed, had been laid out for him. In his dreams he knew what was now confusing would one day become clear.

12

2 WEEKS LATER

Sheriff Dablo knocked gently on the Hanks' household front door. Mrs. Hanks was sitting in front of her vanity in the bedroom, staring at the bruises on her face. She glanced at the clock, 7:30 a.m. Her husband had beaten both her and Noah harshly the night before. She touched her nose, certain it was broken. She had no doubt it would require a trip to Doctor Yackley's office. She sighed at the thought of asking him to once again say nothing to the authorities. She heard the knock again. Mrs. Hanks gazed out the window. Her eyes landed on the Graham County vehicle that had a large gold star, Graham County Sheriff and 911 written on the side. Despair and hope mixed themselves in her mind. She knew it was Sheriff Dablo's truck parked in front of the house. Marta Hanks glanced into the mirror and spoke to herself in quiet desperation.

"I can't let him see me. He'll know what happened. What am I going to do?"

She got up and peered into Zeb's room. He was just beginning to stir. She spoke to her youngest son in a soft, soothing voice.

"Zeb, honey. Could you get the door? It's Sheriff Dablo. Are you going out to the San Carlos with him today?"

Zeb's eyes opened double wide when he saw the lumps and

bruises on his mother's face. He didn't need to be told what happened.

"Where's Dad?" he asked.

"He took off for Red's Roadhouse late last night. He never came home."

A thought breezed through Zeb's mind. He wished his father was dead.

"Where's Noah?"

"In bed."

"Did Dad beat him too?"

Zeb's mother looked away in shame. A tear trickled down her cheek. This time the knock on the door was louder. She wiped away the tear.

"Please, Zeb, answer the door. Don't make me do it. Please?"

Zeb pulled on some pants and a T-shirt. Barefoot, he ran down the stairs and opened the door. Sheriff Dablo's face carried a solemn and sober look. The expression was one he had never seen during his interactions with the sheriff. It sent a chill down Zeb's spine.

"Is your mom here?" he asked.

"Uh, I think she's still in bed," replied Zeb.

"Would you wake her, please? I need to talk to her."

"She doesn't like to be woke up when she's sleeping," said Zeb.

"It's important. Do as I say, Zeb. Don't ask any more questions."

This time Zeb closely examined Sheriff Dablo's face. He could see that something was wrong, deadly wrong.

"Okay, come in. I'll get her."

Zeb ran upstairs. His mother had closed the door to her bedroom. He tapped gently.

"Come in, Zeb," she whispered.

Zeb saw that she was trying to cover up the bruises on her face with makeup. It helped, but Sheriff Dablo was certain to notice the beating she had taken.

"Sheriff Dablo says its important. I told him you were sleeping. He insisted I wake you up."

"Tell him I'll be right down. I just need a couple more minutes."

She turned back to the mirror and thickened the makeup as Zeb bound down the stairs. Sheriff Dablo was standing in the entryway. He held his cowboy hat in his hands like he was standing outside a church. The look on his face had turned even more somber. Zeb stopped dead in his tracks. Something was terribly wrong. He could feel it in his bones.

"Can I get you something, Sheriff Dablo? A glass of water? Some iced tea?"

"No. Is your mother coming down?"

"She's getting dressed. She'll be right here. Is something the matter?"

"Yes," replied Sheriff Dablo.

"What?"

"I need to talk to your mother."

Zeb noticed it was the second time Sheriff Dablo had said he needed to talk to his mom. If it wasn't something bad, he would have said he wanted to talk to her.

"Is it about my dad?"

Mrs. Hanks walked slowly down the stairs. She was unsteady on her feet. The beating to her head had made her dizzy. When she reached the main floor, she offered Sheriff Dablo a seat in the living room.

"Tea?" she asked.

"Please have a seat, Mrs. Hanks."

"I'll stand, thank you," said Mrs. Hanks, steadying herself on the entryway desk.

"Please sit," insisted Jake.

Reading the sheriff's facial expression, she understood his words were more of a command than a request.

Zeb stood in the doorway, watching, listening, wondering what shoe was about to drop.

"What's this about, Sheriff?" asked Mrs. Hanks.

"I've got some bad news about your husband."

"Did he get arrested for drunk driving again?"

"No, it's nothing that simple."

Mrs. Hanks placed her hand in such fashion that it might cover some of her bruises. Her mind traveled to a dozen bad scenarios.

Sheriff Dablo took a deep breath. He detested delivering this kind of information. It was the worst part of an otherwise good job. This type of news had no good side to it.

"Your husband ran his car into a tree last night. Out by Red's Roadhouse."

"Is he hurt?"

"He's in the hospital. Doctor Yackley said his condition was serious."

"Is he going to live?"

"Doc Yackley says your husband has a chance to pull through."

Mrs. Hanks released a sigh of relief. Zeb's head was spinning.

"That's not the real problem, though."

"What'd he do this time?"

Mrs. Hanks voice was that of a realistic woman. A wife who knew her husband.

Sheriff Dablo had been through the drill with her before. There was no sense in beating around the bush.

"He pulled a heist at the Grab and Go. He brandished a weapon. After the robbery he sped off in his car. That's when he ran into the tree. I'm afraid Judge Dunleavy isn't going to be lenient this time."

Mrs. Hanks gasped. Her husband was a drunken no good cheat who beat his wife and children, but to pull a gun on a defenseless clerk at the Grab and Go? How, why would he do such a thing? She knew that most of the clerks were high school kids or single mothers trying to get their lives together.

"Did he kill anyone?"

Marta Hanks stood up as she asked the question. Her voice was calm, almost too calm. It scared Zeb to hear her speak so easily about what his father might have done. It was almost as though she was expecting to hear that he had committed murder. That thought could not, would not cross the threshold of Zeb's thinking.

Zeb stared at the floor. Nothing seemed real.

"He fired two shots. One hit the clerk in the shoulder. Fortunately, it was a superficial wound. She'll live."

Marta Hanks knees buckled. Jake assisted her as she collapsed into a chair.

Noah had crept downstairs and was standing behind Zeb as the sheriff gave their mom the news. Zeb witnessed the horrifying affect the news had on her. Noah spoke from the doorway.

"I wish he was dead. I hope he goes away for good this time."

Through tears, Marta firmly addressed her oldest son.

"Noah Hanks, we do not speak poorly of your father in this house, no matter what he has done."

Sheriff Dablo turned and saw the bruised and battered face of Noah Hanks.

Noah grabbed his motorcycle keys, stormed out of the house and took off down the road.

"Want me to go after him?" asked Sheriff Dablo.

"No. He's upset. He has a difficult relationship with his father. He'll drive around a while, then come back. He's done this many times before."

"I don't want him hurting himself," replied the sheriff. "Or endangering anyone else."

"My husband is at the hospital, you said?"

"Yes."

"What do I need to do?"

"Get Jonas an attorney. There's no avoiding the fact that he's going to go away this time. Probably for quite a while."

The gravity of the situation suddenly hit Marta with hurricane force. She slumped forward in her chair. All of her strength left her body. Jake and Zeb grabbed her to keep her from falling to the floor. Her sobs and moans came from deep inside. Eventually they became wailing howls of pain. Her marriage had long been a sham. It was only at this moment she accepted that fact. How was she going to raise two teenage boys by herself? Zeb and Jake helped her to a chair. Zeb sat next to his mother. He attempted to console her by rubbing his hand across her back. He felt lost. With just some stupid actions by his father, the world he knew it had turned to dust.

"Southern Arizona Legal Aid will provide an attorney for your husband, if you can't afford one" said Sheriff Dablo.

He handed her a card with the phone number for SALA. She thanked him. When she offered to let him out, he said he would find his own way. Jake had known the Hanks family his whole life. For years he had been certain things might end up this way for Jonas. As a friend of the family, as the Graham County Sheriff and as a man, he saw an outcome that was only going to get worse. But maybe, just maybe with Jonas in prison, the family could make a new start. His heart broke for Marta and the boys.

"I'll stop by in a couple of days to check on you, Zeb and Noah."

"Thanks, Jake. I appreciate your help."

"Make that call to legal aid, sooner rather than later."

Sheriff Dablo tipped the brim of his hat to Mrs. Hanks. As the sheriff walked toward the home's front door, his eyes fell upon Zeb's cowboy hat hanging on a rack. He stopped and ran his fingers across the brim. Sheriff Dablo had given him the hat on the day he last arrested his father. Zeb had already broken it in quite well. Jake hoped it would give Zeb courage to face a terribly uncertain future.

As Sheriff Dablo shut the door, the phone rang. It was Marta's sister, Helen Nazelrod. Since Jake's last election, Helen practically ran the sheriff's office. She knew everything that went on in the county. More importantly, she understood how the sheriff thought, what he wanted and when he needed it.

"Marta, I just got the news. I'll be right over."

"Thank you, Helen. Jake was just here."

"I know. I just talked with him on the two-way radio."

"Don't rush. I'm okay."

"No, you're not. I'm on my way. You shouldn't be alone at a time like this."

Marta broke down, sobbing.

"I, I just don't know what to do. I feel like I'm frozen in pain. I hate Jonas for doing this to, to everyone," said Marta.

"Marta don't let the devil ride on your anger. It will ruin you and the boys. I'll be right over. We can pray. We can drink tea. I can help you figure out what to do next. It's a hard time, but hard times always pass."

Five minutes later Helen let herself into the Hanks' house. Marta collapsed in her sister's arms. Zeb watched it all. He saw the hurt. He felt the betrayal. He was lost in the confusion of everything swirling around him. Yet, because of his age and inexperience, he understood little of the depths of emotions that were filling the room.

Two months later Jonas Hanks was sentenced to serve 7-10 years at the Marana Community Correctional Treatment Facility (MCCTF). Jonas had convinced the judge, a reformed alcoholic himself, that he could change his ways if he got the help he needed with the proper program for alcohol addiction. For that reason, he sentenced Jonas to MCCTF. At that facility he could get the treatment he needed. The minimum-security prison held 500 inmates. All of them demonstrated a need for the treatment of alcohol and substance abuse.

At the sentencing, Judge Dunleavy lectured Jonas on the need to stay the course. If he did, he might see his family in just under four years.

"You will miss some of the most precious time in your sons' lives. It is a shame you chose to live your life in a such a fashion that led to this point. But, if you reform yourself, you will be setting a good example for your boys. Good luck. Don't screw it up. I'm trusting that I made the right decision about your life and its future. Follow the twelve-step program. Don't even think about deviating from it."

Judge Dunleavy slammed his gavel. The noise echoed in Zeb's ears. Jonas was allowed one last hug for each of his family members that were present. Noah had refused to go to the sentencing. Zeb hugged his trembling dad. The embrace seemed hollow, as though he were hugging someone he didn't even know. Zeb suddenly realized his father was mostly a stranger. As Marta, with tears watering her eyes, put her arms around the man she married and had two children with, she realized he didn't smell like himself, nor did he feel like her husband. Intuitively, she knew their relationship was over and done. Zeb stuck his hands in the pockets of his jeans and watched stoically as the guards led his handcuffed father away. He decided he would visit whenever his mother did, if only to make the burden easier on her. As Jonas Hanks passed through the door, back to the jail, Zeb and his mother had the same thought. Life was not going to be the same. In fact, nothing was going to be left unchanged.

13

2 MONTHS LATER

Noah answered the ringing phone.

"Just a sec. I'll get her."

Marta called out.

"Who is it?"

"It's some guy from the MCCTF in Marana."

The mere mention of the name of the prison where Jonas was serving his time sent shivers up and down Marta's spine. The person on the other end of the line told Noah who he was. He quickly relayed the information.

"It's Warden Moyer. Says he needs to talk to you."

A strange, unsettled feeling enveloped Marta as she picked up the phone. The warden had never called before. What could he possibly want?

"I'll pick it up in the kitchen. You can hang up."

Noah listened, hanging up when his mother spoke.

"This is Marta Hanks."

"This is Warden Moyer, from the Marana Community Correctional Treatment Facility."

"Yes, Warden Moyer. How may I help you?"

"I'm sorry to be delivering this news to you..."

Marta's heart fluttered. Her knees weakened.

"Yes?"

"Your husband was injured in a prison fight last night."

"Is he...all right?" asked Marta.

"He's on his way by ambulance to the Banner Medical Center. I think you should get over there," said Warden Moyer.

"Is he all right?"

Marta knew in her heart her husband was not all right.

"He's going to need emergency surgery."

"Is he going to be all right?"

"I'm not a doctor and the nurse who attended to him didn't know how severe the injury actually was. In short, I don't have enough information to answer your question."

Marta buried her face in here hands. When she came up for air, she was livid with rage.

"What happened? At least you can tell me that."

Nearby, Zeb was all ears. The sound of his mother's voice told him she was upset. Her being in such a state created a bad feeling in his gut.

"I can tell you this much. He was involved in a fight that involved homemade weapons. In prison their called shivs. He was stabbed."

"Where? In the leg? In the chest?"

"In the belly."

"He's not dead. He's still alive, right?"

"Yes, as far as I know. He was alive when he was put into the ambulance. I'm waiting to hear from the hospital. I'll let you know what is going on as soon as I know."

"I'm leaving right now for Tucson."

"Do you know where the Banner Medical Center is?" asked Warden Moyer.

"Yes, of course."

"Surgery for prisoners is done on the east wing of the fourth floor. I'll be there when you get there."

Marta hung up without saying goodbye. Instantly she began to sweat and tremble. She recognized she was having a panic attack. It was not her first. It wouldn't be her last.

"Zeb, get your brother and get in the car. Do it now!"

Noah said nothing on the road to Tucson. Zeb did his best to calm his mother. But Marta Hanks was flush with the ill sentiments that accompany anxiety and panic. Warden Moyer was waiting for them outside the surgical arena. He walked directly to Marta and asked her to sit.

"What's the matter?" asked Marta.

"Please. Sit."

"He's dead, isn't he?"

"I'm sorry."

Marta exploded into tears. Her emotions ran the gamut from pain to relief before circling back to pain and settling there. The warden sat down next to her. He spoke calmly and from his heart.

"Jonas lost too much blood. He didn't survive the surgery. I'm terribly sorry."

The surgeon emerged from the surgical arena, still gloved up and in her scrubs. She walked up to Marta and explained that she had done her best to save Jonas. However, the wound had punctured multiple organs and severed the abdominal artery.

"He bled to death?" asked Marta.

Zeb and Noah began to cry.

"I am so sorry," said the doctor. "My team and I did all we could to save his life. The loss of blood was too great for him to sustain life."

"Thank you for trying," said Marta. "I appreciate that you did what you could."

The warden had disappeared, gone to find the chaplain. The pair returned just as the surgeon departed.

"I'm Reverend Eldon Luther. My sincerest apologies for your loss. Would you like to talk?"

Everything was happening so fast. Marta's head was spinning. She did not know what to think. She did not know what it was that she was feeling. She was lost in a lost world.

"Are these young men your sons?" asked Reverend Luther.

Marta nodded.

"Why don't you all come with me to the lounge. We can talk."

Noah responded by shouting at Reverend Luther through his tears.

"There's not a goddamned thing you can do to help us. He's dead. D-E-A-D. Dead."

"Noah, stop that right now."

Marta Hanks was teetering on the edge of an abyss. Noah's anger was not helping the situation.

"Shut up, Noah," whispered Zeb.

Noah slugged Zeb so hard it spun him in a circle. Zeb barely felt the pain of the punch. Reverend Luther grabbed Noah and held him, hugged him.

"I know, son. It's terrible what you are feeling."

"You have no idea what I'm feeling. I'm glad he's dead."

"Noah. Please stop," pleaded Mrs. Hanks.

"It's okay," said Reverend Luther. "He's upset."

Noah wrestled himself out of the reverend's grip.

"Please, this way," said Reverend Luther.

What was left of the Hanks' immediate family entered a private room. Marta broke an uncomfortable silence.

"What do I do now?" she asked.

"I'll help with the arrangements. Perhaps you'd like to talk first?"

"No," replied Marta. "I've been half-expecting something like this would happen."

Zeb and Noah were stunned by their mother's remark. She had said nothing of that sort to them.

"Then perhaps we should call your Pastor?"

"We're Mormon. Could you call Bishop Behunin in Safford and tell him what's happened? That would be a great help."

Zeb and Noah could not believe how calm their mother was acting. From memory Marta gave Bishop Behunin's number. The Reverend Luther and Bishop Behunin spoke for a matter of minutes in which all the necessary information was exchanged. Fifteen minutes later, all that needed to be done was to have the body sent to the Kayita and Townes funeral home in Safford. The rest of the arrangements would be made.

Three days later Noah and Zeb drove to the graveyard. Noah had a strange desire to watch Marcus Bren, the local gravedigger, dig the grave. He grabbed Zeb and told him to come along. Straddling their bikes, the boys stood outside the graveyard's perimeter fence.

"He does them all by hand," said Noah.

Zeb watched. His emotions bounced all over the place until Noah said what he really had to say.

"He's never gonna beat Momma or me ever again."

Jonas Hanks was buried in the Church of Jesus Christ of the Latter-Day Saints area of the Safford public cemetery. Few, if any, tears were shed.

As the Hanks family departed the burial, Noah turned to Zeb and whispered.

"This is what justice looks like."

"I know," replied Zeb. "I know."

PART II

14

THE FUTURE BECKONS

"Zeb, I understand you're leaving us," said Angus McGinty.

"Yes, sir. I wanted to come to your office and personally thank you for the opportunity to learn about the mining business and to save some money for a truck."

A summer of manual labor at the Danforth-Roerg copper mine and an unwanted sexual approach by Lily McGinty, Angus' wife, helped Zeb make up his mind about moving on.

"What are your plans, young man?"

"I'm heading off tomorrow for United States Border Patrol training. They call it Border Boot Camp."

"I'm aware," said Angus.

"Why did you choose that? If you stay here, I can move you up the ladder. You'll make significantly more money than you will by being simply a border patrol agent."

"Becoming a border patrol agent feels like a calling in some strange way," said Zeb.

"A calling? You want to help desperate people trying to illegally enter the United States of America? Or, do you want to enforce the law as it is written?"

"I did some work with the border patrol when I was in Explorer

Scouts. I liked it, all parts of it. The opportunity came up and, well, I took it. Don't get me wrong. Working for Danforth-Roerg was a great stepping stone into the future. But what lies ahead for me in terms of a career seems like it should be law enforcement."

"Have you talked this over with Sheriff Dablo?"

"Actually, he was the one who suggested I apply for the job. He thought it would give me a foot up on a career. Being a CBP agent is a stepping stone into other areas of law."

"Good," replied Angus. "You sound like you've got your head screwed on right."

"Once again, I want to thank you for the opportunity for working in the mines, sir."

"We'll miss you around here, but a man has to do what a man has to do," replied Angus. "My wife seems to have taken a particular attraction to you. I don't know if that's a good thing or a bad thing."

"Yes, sir," replied Zeb.

Angus McGinty stuck out his hand. Zeb gave him a manly handshake. He breathed a sigh of relief. Angus must not have known about the sexually aggressive manner in which his wife approached Zeb.

"Your job is always open if you want to come back," said Angus.

"Thank you, sir, but I think my future lies somewhere other than Safford."

Angus McGinty stepped back and gave Zeb a quick study.

"You may well feel that way today. Youth has its own unique perspective. But I suspect one day Safford will be your town."

Zeb shook Angus' hand, turned heel, flipped on his cowboy hat and felt the relief of a man who had just been set free.

15

BORDER PATROL

The training to become a United States Customs and Border Protection (CBP) agent was less difficult for Zeb than filling out the nine-page application form. At the first day of classes, he took a seat in the back row like he always had in high school. The instructor promptly moved all the men and women who took the back seats to the front of the room and those in the front were moved to the back.

"If people in my class hide in the back row, I need to keep an eye on them. If they scramble for the front seats, I am suspicious they are seeking favoritism."

Zeb sat at attention. He knew it was the best way to go unnoticed.

"The CBP is one of the largest law enforcement organizations in the world. We make thousands of apprehensions and seize tons of illegal drugs every day. We need men and women..."

Zeb glanced around the room. Of the thirty people in his class, three were women.

"...with the integrity it takes to serve on the frontline. How many military veterans do I have in this class? Raise your hands."

Over half the class raised their hands.

"Good. That tells me you already understand a sense of duty. The pay is good, time off is excellent and career opportunities are incredible. On top of that, health and life insurance are offered to you, and the retirement program is far better than the private sector. Don't tell the taxpayers about that one."

The class collectively chuckled.

"After preliminary training you can specialize in a K-9 Unit, Inspection, become a part of the Special Response Team, work on Horse Patrol, Bike Patrol, Off-road Vehicle Unit Patrol or become a member of the Anti-Terrorism Contraband Enforcement Team."

Zeb saw himself on the Contraband Enforcement Team, mostly because he had seen the devastation drugs had brought to Graham County and the surrounding counties. But the horseback unit seemed like a good possibility as well.

"You will complete a nineteen-week resident course with instruction in integrated law, physical training, firearms instruction, driving and, of course, Spanish language. Nine out of ten people you apprehend will speak only Spanish. You will be trained at the Border Patrol Agent Academy. You must obtain a minimum overall average of seventy percent in all your courses."

The instructor spoke without interruption for six hours. Everything he talked about seemed doable. Zeb was eager to start his training and get to work.

The nineteen weeks went by quickly. On graduation day, with his mother at his side, Zeb received his United States Border Patrol Agent certification. His first assignment was the eastern Arizona border. He knew the area well and was excited to become a member of a Contraband Enforcement Team.

His first few weeks as a U.S. Border Patrol Agent were routine. Then one night everything changed when the intensity ratcheted up several notches. Zeb was working with Agent Melendez. Melendez had five years of experience tucked under his belt and loved his work. Zeb noted three main details about his partner. He seemed fearless, but not foolishly so. Second, he appeared exceptionally wealthy for a man in his twenties. He had a brand-new truck, fancy boots, an expansive new house and spent money like water flowing from a spring time river. The third thing was that Melendez counted Senator Clinton Jefferson Russell among his friends. Zeb found that an odd coupling.

"We've got actionable intelligence that says a coyote is moving twenty-two people through our zone tonight. You ready for some action, Agent Hanks?" asked Agent Melendez.

Everything Zeb had learned in class about coyotes popped into his head. In the food chain of bad guys, they ranked near the top. They took money to bring illegals across the border and often held a family member, usually a child, as a hostage. They use the child to extort more money from the people who were paying them to help them illegally cross the border. Coyotes also sold children into prostitution. That bothered Zeb deeply. The coyotes frequently carried weapons. That was to be expected. But more often than not, when confronted by CBP agents, they would jump and run leaving the illegals to fend for themselves. If the coyotes were armed and fired on CBP agents, it usually meant they were muling drugs along with the people.

"Here. Put this on. I smell trouble."

Agent Melendez reached into the back seat and handed Zeb his body armor.

"Never forget that your body armor is bullet resistant. It sure as hell ain't bulletproof."

"We learned that in training," replied Zeb.

"Never been shot at, have you?"

"No, sir. I have not."

"I've been hit twice. Both times they were angular blows from handguns. Each time I ended up with broken ribs. The body armor won't help a lick if you get shot from within fifty yards or so with a high-powered rifle. If you see someone pointing a rifle at you, take cover. Don't be a dead hero."

Zeb slipped into his vest. Five minutes later, using night vision goggles, they spotted a string of over twenty people moving through the desert brush.

"See their backpacks?" asked Melendez.

"Yes," said Zeb, studying the group through military grade thermal imaging binoculars.

"Oversized," said Melendez.

"Drugs, right?" said Zeb, regurgitating his training.

"Yes, rookie. You got it. Now, have a second look and see if you spot any weapons, long guns in particular."

Zeb saw none.

"Should we call in backup?" asked Zeb.

Melendez tapped on his dashboard screen. Three red dots were positioned in such a way to surround the illegals.

"The cavalry has already arrived and is in position. Everything is routine."

In his excitement and nervousness, Zeb had forgotten to check the screen. He kicked himself for his rookie mistake.

"What do we do now?" asked Zeb.

"Archer is head of the detail tonight. He'll give us a go signal when we've got them trapped."

The adrenaline raced through Zeb's veins. He checked his weapon. Melendez noticed.

"Don't get trigger happy. Look again. Take your time. Look closely."

The illegals had moved closer into view, giving Zeb better eyes on the situation.

"Kids," said Zeb. "They've put kids in the front, back and middle of the pack."

"Right. Kill a kid and you'll be on the six o'clock news. Plus, your career will be over quicker than it began."

"Got it."

"One more thing," said Melendez. "And remember this as if your life depended on it. Because it does."

"Yeah?"

"Never, and I mean never, cross swords with Archer."

Zeb broke into a sweat for a couple of good reasons. The last thing he wanted to do was hurt a child, much less kill one. His training had downplayed the possibility of that happening. As to Archer, the man in charge of the operation, he knew very little. But he did know that Archer had served in some secret branch of military Special Forces and was feared by everyone who had contact with him. Zeb had seen Archer around during his training. He seemed like the proverbial little guy who liked to act tough.

"You nervous yet, Cowboy?" asked Melendez, grinning.

Zeb had earned the nickname, Cowboy, because he had come to training every day wearing his cowboy hat

"Some."

"Good. I hate to think you were so stupid that you weren't at least a little bit nervous," replied Melendez.

The dots surrounding the illegals turned from red to green. This was the classic go signal for the border patrol agents.

"Ready to rock and roll?"

"Yup," replied Zeb. "As ready as I know how to be."

"Just like sex, the first time is always the hardest. Follow my lead and you'll be good."

"Thanks."

"Thank me later with a cerveza," replied Melendez.

Fifteen minutes later twenty illegals were sitting in the desert sand with hands bound behind their backs. Two others had fled. Archer and his partner were in hot pursuit of the runners. Shortly thereafter, what sounded like a brief gun battle ensued. Ten minutes later Archer and his partner pulled up with the two men. One man was dead. The other was bleeding.

"Medic," shouted Archer half-heartedly.

The team medic ran to Archer. Zeb was standing nearby and overheard their conversation. Even though the medic was in direct line of the injured man, he awaited orders from Archer before acting. Archer pointed to the men he and his partner had brought in.

"That one's dead. That one can use your help. Take your time easing his pain. I'd like you to get some intel from him before he's out of discomfort."

The medic went to work. Within minutes the injured man was handing over information as fast as it could be translated.

"Somebody call in a van to haul these assholes out of here?" asked Archer.

"Yes, sir," replied Melendez.

"Melendez, who's your partner, the new guy?"

"Agent Zebulon P. Hanks."

"Hanks, help Melendez keep everyone in order. You've got thirty minutes to get these people out of here. Everyone else, get back to your nightly details. We've got nothing else that's hot right now. Stay alert. These guys weren't carrying enough drugs or money for this to be from the Sandoval Cartel. I know how El Chapo operates. This is just some small crew trying to make the most of the recent Mexican cartel infighting."

Archer, his partner and the other two vehicles disappeared over a hill and into the desert night.

"How does Archer know these guys aren't Sandoval cartel?" asked Zeb.

Melendez chuckled.

"He knows. That's all that matters."

An hour later, after the twenty captured illegals had been handed off, Melendez and Zeb continued their duty.

"Is it like this on busy nights?" asked Zeb.

"Do you mean do we often arrest decent sized groups of people?"

"Yeah. How often is there this kind of action?" asked Zeb.

"There is always something going down. There is also always too much waiting around. Rarely are any shots fired...unless Archer is around. He likes to heat up the action. It's his nature."

"Is that good or bad?" asked Zeb.

Melendez shrugged his shoulders.

"Depends on your point of view."

Zeb pulled a small notebook from his shirt pocket and made some notes.

"Afraid you'll forget something?" asked Melendez.

"Just making a few notes on how things work," replied Zeb.

Melendez just shook his head and muttered, "Rookie."

"I'm trying to learn," said Zeb. "I want to understand the process as completely as I possibly can."

"Then you'll want to write this down. Tomorrow night we've got a ride along."

"Who?" asked Zeb.

The Cheshire cat could not have grinned as satisfyingly.

"You'll see."

16

SENATOR RUSSELL

THE NEXT NIGHT

"Ready for our ride along?" asked Agent Melendez.

"You going to let me know who it is?" asked Zeb. "I'm guessing it's a political do-gooder looking to make sure we do our jobs the right way."

"No. This time it's different. But you are right about the political part."

"Who is it?" asked Zeb.

"Senator Clinton Jefferson Russell," replied Melendez.

"What's going on?" asked Zeb.

"Don't know, but I hear it's a good thing."

A black SUV pulled up outside the CBP station. A man who appeared to be in his mid-forties stepped out. He was dressed in ill-fitting military fatigues that looked perfectly wrong on him. Along with his driver, there were a pair of bodyguards. Zeb immediately recognized the senator. Agents Melendez and Hanks departed their vehicle to greet him.

"Sir, good to have you on board," said Melendez.

"Good to see you again, Julio. How's the wife and family?" asked Senator Russell.

"All is well on the home front. The wife says hello."

"My wife enjoyed entertaining your family at our estate last summer. Perhaps we should all get together again soon?"

"Yes, sir. That would be great."

Senator Russell turned to Zeb.

"Are you going to introduce me to your new partner?" asked Senator Russell, nodding at Zeb.

"This is Agent Zebulon Hanks."

Zeb extended a hand to the senator. The senator's hands were soft and pudgy. He knew Senator Russell had grown up in the Safford area and kept a ranch there. Zeb had no prior contact with him.

"Zeb Hanks, Safford baseball pitcher who almost led the Tigers into the state tournament last year, right?"

"Yes, sir," replied Zeb.

"I follow the Tigers, believe it or not. I read about that bunt you laid down in the district championship game. Well done. I like a man who works outside the box. I really like a man who's a team player."

"Thank you, sir."

"Tonight, you men can call me Clint, like Clint Eastwood."

The agents smiled. Senator Russell was barely over five and a half feet tall, balding, chubby and had thick, clumsy fingers. He was hardly a Clint Eastwood prototype.

"Let's get to work. I want to see what you boys do for a living and how the taxpayers' money is being spent."

The night was easy. A few pickups of illegals. A lone wolf carrying five kilos of heroin. An abandoned vehicle with traces of cocaine in the trunk. Nothing out of the ordinary. By two a.m. Senator Russell was tired and wanted to call it a night. He called his car to meet them. Before he departed he spoke to Agents Melendez and Hanks.

"Agent Melendez."

"Yes, sir, I mean, yes, Clint."

Senator Russell handed Melendez a card.

"You interested in working for the FBI?"

"Yes. That is my career goal."

"Call the man whose name is on that card. My initials are on the back. Tell him I told you to contact him. Set up an appointment.

Don't wait. Do it tomorrow. Give him the card when you meet him. You should be in like Flynn. Good luck."

"Thank you, Senator Russell."

"My pleasure, Agent Melendez. You've come highly recommended."

"Agent Hanks."

"Yes, Clint."

Zeb felt odd addressing such an important man so casually. It didn't fit in with the manners his mother, Sheriff Dablo and Medicine Man Jimmy Song Bird had taught him.

"I read your dossier."

"Sir?"

"It seems a fast track in the Tucson Police Department is more suited to your skills. Would you agree?"

"I have been thinking about moving into police work."

"I chatted with Sheriff Dablo. He thought you might be interested in serving a local community," said Senator Russell.

"I am."

Senator Russell handed Zeb a card.

"Call this person. She handles HR for the police department in Tucson. If you want the job, it's yours."

Senator Russell stepped out of the CBP vehicle and into his SUV. Agents Julio Melendez and Zeb Hanks looked at each other, wondering what had just happened.

"Didn't he mean in like Flint?" asked Zeb.

"Senator Russell is old school. He meant in like Flynn, as in the great actor, Errol Flynn. That's where the saying originated."

Zeb was stunned by his partner's apparent knowledge of such an obscure point.

"You going to move to Tucson, rookie?" asked Melendez.

"I think so," replied Zeb. "For sure I'm going to check it out."

"You going to take that FBI job?" asked Zeb.

"Hell, yes. When I hear opportunity knocking, I open up the door."

17

TUCSON POLICE DEPARTMENT

6 WEEKS LATER

"Zeb Hanks, welcome to the Tucson Police Department."

Zeb took a seat in front of Sargeant Maximilian Muñoz's desk.

"How well do you know Tucson?"

"I know my way around. I don't know the city like the back of my hand or anything like that."

"I see you're from Safford."

"Yes, sir."

"Easy on the sir stuff. In front of senior officers, yes, but when we're one on one, it's not necessary. Call me Max."

"Thanks, Max. I never know what to expect from big city folks."

Max chuckled.

"Me neither."

Zeb's puzzled look made Max laugh even louder.

"Big city? You ever heard of Double Adobe."

"Er, no. Maybe. No, it doesn't ring a bell. Should I have heard of it?"

"It's in Arizona. As the crow flies, it's seventy-five miles from Safford. Two hundred long miles if you take the paved roads."

Zeb scrunched his eyebrows.

"It's my hometown," explained Max. "Blink and you'll miss it. It's so small we use the same sign for when you're entering and when you're leaving town. So, let's not have any of that big city boy stuff with me."

Zeb felt immediately at ease. He was among his own.

"Looks like I'm going to be your boss, at least for a while."

"Good," replied Zeb.

"I also want to be up front with you. I'm on a fast track to detective. A guy from Gleeson, another whistle stop town that's even smaller than Double Adobe, helped me out. If you like the work and find yourself interested, I'll do the same for you. You know how it goes, if you get a break, you should give someone a break. Right?"

Zeb nodded. He knew Gleeson and he agreed with Max's point of view.

"I can't argue with that philosophy."

"I've been looking for someone I could trust. It might take a while for me to get a good word in for you and get you in the fast track program. I've got to see how you operate first."

"Fair enough. Can I ask, why me?" inquired Zeb.

"Your record with the CBP, although it's not a lengthy one, and your recommendations are top of the line. But that's not your ticket, at least not in my book."

"Then what is?"

"Baseball."

"Baseball?"

"I followed the Safford Tigers and actually went to the district championship game you played against the Bisbee Bees a few years back. Any slugger who is willing to lay down a bunt when it really counts is a team man. I need team men, not cowboys."

Zeb chuckled.

"Yes?" asked Max.

"I take it that it isn't in my report that my nickname at the CBP was Cowboy?"

Zeb tipped up his ever-present cowboy hat. This time it was Max's turn to laugh.

"Okay, Cowboy. And, by the way, your nickname is in your file."

"I'll do my best to be a team player," said Zeb.

"Good. Your first assignment is a part of Tucson known as Little Village aka Pequeña Villa."

"My Español, even with the CBP training, is not so hot, so let's call it Little Village."

"Let's make it even easier by calling it what most people call it– The Village."

"I can do that. Give me the skinny on The Village."

"It's an area that used to be run by the Chinese mafia back in the day when the railroad was first built here. The Chinese ran it for almost a century. The Chinese moved to a middle-class part of town and the Mexican gangs took it over. Now it's an Indian/Mexican/Chinese drug ghetto. It's the roughest part of Tucson. I remembered your baseball team was made up of Mexican and Indian kids. With that in mind, you seemed like a reasonable fit for The Village. I also read in your dossier a recommendation from a medicine man on the San Carlos reservation, Jimmy Song Bird, I believe. Graham County Sheriff Jake Dablo's high praise didn't hurt you any either."

"Yes, they both mentored me before and after my father was killed in prison."

"I read about your father in your file as well. Rough deal."

"He died like he lived. Some things are inevitable."

Maximilian and Zeb sat quietly in the type of stony silence that forms the foundation of a friendship. Sargeant Muñoz eventually broke the silence.

"I am assigning you to work with Officer Lipana Torones. He knows the beat. He's been working it for a year, almost two really. Plus, he grew up in the area. He's a former gang banger. He's tougher than nails and stands about six-foot ten. He's got a scar across his mug that makes him look dangerous. He's really kind of a pussycat, and definitely one of the nicest people I've ever met."

"Sounds like a good man to work with," said Zeb.

"He's got plenty of informants, including a confidential informant who's knows the inner workings of the Sandoval cartel."

"Good. That should be helpful."

"Helpful but damn dangerous."

Zeb nodded. He had not worked that much with CIs, but he had heard they were generally the kind of people who had nothing to lose. That, and they knew how to play the system to their advantage.

"Lipana stays inside the law but operates near its edges. Learn from him. The more you learn from him the faster I can move you up the hierarchy."

"Got it."

"One final thing."

"Yes?"

"Lipana works a little too close with the FBI for my liking. I don't know how you feel about interagency cooperation, but if the FBI has a chance to grab the glory and let you do the work, they will. Never forget that. I don't know how or what Lipana's deal is with the FBI, but it's the real deal. He knows someone in the Bureau who feeds him information."

"Any idea who it is? I mean, in case I hear a name mentioned."

"I have heard inklings that he has a working relationship with an agent by the name of Rodriguez. I don't know what Lipana is giving back in return. I have a gut feeling that Rodriguez is not to be trusted. That being said, I suspect it will take a while for you to get to know how he operates. Lipana's prior partners never could figure out how he managed to play all sides of the scene and always come out so squeaky clean."

Zeb tapped his forehead.

"Got it. Notched into my memory."

A few hours later Zeb and Lipana 'Too Tall' Torones were patrolling the area known as The Village, or, as Lipana called it, Pequeña Villa. Safford had a poor area known as Little Mexico, but it was nothing like this. Little Mexico, in Zeb's hometown, was the home of hard-working laborers who happened to be low income. Crime in Little Mexico was no different than crime in the entirety of Graham County. The situation in the Village looked much more dire.

"I've been working with one of my informants," said Lipana. "He's ballsy."

"What do you mean?"

"No one talks openly and freely about the new cartel. But, for some reason, he's giving me first hand info on how this new cartel is operating."

"Yeah? Any idea why he's being so open with you."

"They're using kids. He doesn't like that," said Lipana.

"How are they using them?" asked Zeb.

"As everything from lookouts and dealers to runners and even drug mules."

"Smart," replied Zeb. "Kids can be playing and act as lookouts. How would you ever know what they were up to? I suppose they use kids as dealers because you can't prosecute a thirteen or fourteen-year-old on a drug felony without him being back on the street by eighteen at the latest."

"Like I said, the new cartel gangsters are smart. They run their operations like businesses. They know how to use the law to their advantage. The Capos ..."

"Capos?"

"The gang lord. The man who runs the whole shebang."

"Gotcha."

"Think of them like a corporate CEO. One huge difference is that they don't mind using children, guns and killing people. The grapevine says that they are teaching kids as young as nine years old how to use automatic weapons. The world is changing fast."

"Question," said Zeb.

"Shoot," replied Lipana.

"How are they using kids as drug mules? I worked with the CBP for the better part of two years and that was never part of their modus operandi."

"Stuffed animals," replied Lipana.

"How's that work?" asked Zeb.

"You must've busted a group that had kids in it?"

"Yeah. Frequently."

"When you busted a family group, were the parents carrying backpacks full of cocaine or heroin?"

"Yup. Far too common of an occurrence. It put the kids in serious danger. None of us liked that. The idea of hurting an innocent child, well, you know, it's a nightmare scenario," said Zeb.

"How often did you take a teddy bear from a scared, crying kid?"

"We were ordered not to."

"Who gave the order?"

"Captain Archer gave it to my partner, Melendez. I followed suit."

"Archer is dirty, really dirty. Melendez is suspected of making a lot of cash working the dark side too."

"I knew Archer was corrupt. How could I have missed Melendez?" asked Zeb.

"My informant knows everyone at the border. He knows who's dirty. He knows who's clean. He knows you're clean."

"You had me checked out?"

Too Tall Lipana raised his eyebrows and smiled.

"How does your guy have so much inside dope?"

"Years of working a ton of connections. Plus, he's an insider who's never been suspected of anything that would piss off the cartel."

"How can he know that I'm not dirty?"

"You'd have been talked about. Every cartel guy knows what government agents are working with them."

"How dirty is Archer?"

"In my world view, he's filthy. Archer is protected from both sides of the border. He's working with El Coyote south of the border..."

"El Coyote? I thought El Coyote was a Mexican cartel myth."

"He's as real as you or me. He's been at it a long time, and his cartel is just now becoming one of the really heavy hitters. You could say he recently got promoted from single A ball to the big leagues."

Zeb smiled at the baseball reference. Lipana continued his explanation.

"El Coyote uses lots of ex-military people from both the U.S. and

Mexico. Half his guys have seen action in Afghanistan or Iraq. They're tough. They don't crack under pressure, and they understand teamwork."

"Who's protecting El Coyote north of the border?"

"Word on the street is that somebody, an elected official in Washington, is his godfather."

"Who?"

"No one seems to know. It could be only a rumor. It could be true. My informant doesn't know...yet. He's spending a lot of his goodwill digging into it."

"Your CI really is ballsy."

"He did a couple of tours in the sandbox."

"Army?"

"Black-ops. He's both smart and tough. He also did some time in Afghanistan as an independent contractor."

"After all that, how did he end up back in the gang business?"

"He told me when he got home his head was all fucked up. He needed money for a bunch of things, including what might be considered a well-earned heroin habit. I'm sure you know Afghanistan is where most of the world's heroin originates. That's how he got involved. He was assigned to a Cobra team that provided overwatch protection for the Afghan National Police who help protect the poppy fields. He was a little too close to the product, and it didn't cost him anything. Who knows how a heroin habit begins, but an active war zone is a pretty common starting spot."

"When you combine war and drugs, you've got really dirty business," said Zeb.

"You got that right. When he got back to the real world, one of his former black-ops team members recruited him for the cartel. Working for El Coyote was the quickest way to get what he needed, the heroin, and what he wanted, to be part of a team again."

"Shit happens."

"Yes, it does."

"I've heard El Coyote's people don't take prisoners. Is that a rumor or is it the truth?" asked Zeb.

"If you're part of the cartel or a Mexican national and you fuck up, you are dead meat. If you're an American, you have a small chance of being negotiated out of a bad scene, under certain circumstances. El Coyote had my CI's best buddy, the guy who recruited him into the cartel, executed six months ago. My CI is off the skag now. His head is clear, and he wants to take El Coyote down for killing his buddy. He doesn't give a shit about much of anything other than seeing El Coyote six feet underground. He's got a bad case of needing to get payback for his buddy. We call it the payback blues."

"Are you going to have me meet your CI?"

"Not now. I don't know you well enough...yet. He doesn't know you at all. It's tricky. Learn the system as fast as you can. It won't take you long to learn why I can't introduce the two of you just yet."

"Fair enough," replied Zeb. "And I will learn the system as fast as I can."

"Let's get some work done," said Lipana.

"There's no time like the present," replied Zeb.

"Got that right, Cowboy."

18

BAD DEAL GONE DOWN

30 MONTHS LATER

"Time flies when you're having fun. Doesn't it, fast tracker?" asked Lipana.

Zeb let Lipana's remark about being a fast tracker slide. In the two plus years since he had been on the fast track not much forward progress toward becoming a detective had been made. In fact, his buddy Max Muñoz had only a few months earlier gotten into the program.

"It's been a hell of a ride. I've learned a ton," replied Zeb. "I owe you."

Zeb was behind the wheel of the unmarked car as it made the turn into the outer perimeter of the Village.

"I must be a good teacher because you've lasted longer than any of my other partners, even your buddy Max Muñoz."

"You worked with Muñoz? I've been working with you and been friends with him for over two years and neither of you have ever mentioned that you worked together. What's that all about?"

"Didn't want it getting in the way," said Lipana.

"Have you kept in touch with Muñoz the whole time we've been working together?" asked Zeb.

Lipana held his thumb and first finger about two inches apart.

"That's how big his file is on you, at least from what I've fed him."

"You did a good job hiding it."

"He wanted to make sure if he helped fast track you to detective that you'd earned it," said Lipana.

"Have I?" asked Zeb.

"In my opinion you have," replied Lipana. "But my opinion and a few greenbacks will get you an iced coffee at Starbucks."

"How come you haven't worked yourself up the ladder?" asked Zeb.

"These are my people."

Lipana held his hands palm up and gestured to the surrounding area.

"Pequeña Villa is my place. I can do a lot of good here. Detective work, having only a few cases at a time, is just not my cup of tea."

They drove into the dark heart of the Village. Something big, something strange was in the air. After a year in the confines of Tucson's crime district, Zeb had a hardened but insightful feel for the place.

"Want to meet my CI?" asked Lipana. "I think it's time."

"I do want to meet him. And it is about time," replied Zeb.

"We're going to bust a medium sized dealer who goes by the name of Germano. He's picking up thirty pounds of heroin at a warehouse on Fifty-sixth and Wabasha. You can take credit for things on our end. It'll push you up the fast track faster," laughed Lipana.

"Is it one of El Coyote's men we're taking down?" asked Zeb.

"Fuck yes," replied Lipana. "Down and dirty. El Coyote's man is more than just another guy. It's El Coyote's brother. He won't be traveling light. If we nab him, it'll put us one step closer to El Coyote himself."

"I assume that even though it's an eleventh-hour operation, that we've got plenty of back-up?" asked Zeb.

"Yes, of course. Muñoz is running point on the operation."

Even though Muñoz had been working on it for months, the actual take down was a last-minute situation. Things were moving fast. Lipana had only found out about the deal an hour before their shift started. Even to Muñoz the timing of it all had come as a surprise. Muñoz and his team, working with information the CI had given them, wanted the dealer for many things, including multiple murders. The CI knew El Coyote would become irrational and probably do something stupid if his brother got nailed. Everyone on the team was hoping that would cause El Coyote to make himself vulnerable.

"Muñoz kept us out of the loop. In fact, he kept just about everyone on the outside because he truly believes the unknown insider from D.C. has their fingerprints all over this one. If Max had created any trail, paper or otherwise, this is the kind of thing that could go sideways in a flash."

"It makes for a dangerous situation for everyone involved," said Zeb.

"You got that right. If the big-time player in D.C. got wind of things, I guess he could make Muñoz vanish in a heartbeat. Got it?" said Lipana. "The only animal more dangerous than a cartel lord is a powerful politico."

"How much backup are we getting?"

"Eight officers. Four officers and four detectives. Plus, my CI will be there."

"How will I ID your CI?" asked Zeb.

Lipana smiled.

"He'll be wearing a Safford Tigers baseball shirt and hat."

Zeb smiled at the irony.

"Remember," added Lipana. "Never shoot a guy from the home team."

Zeb had been in on more than a dozen good-sized heroin, methamphetamine and cocaine busts. With Lipana he had made seizures big enough to make the six o'clock news on numerous occasions. Together they had made over a hundred smaller busts. Both knew how the other man worked, how they thought and how they would react in any given situation. This arrest and confiscation of thirty pounds of heroin was meant to put enough of a hurt on El Coyote's cartel to dim his rising star status. At Lipana's suggestion, Zeb parked the unmarked patrol car in an alley behind a run-down, vacant house.

"We'll walk from here," said Lipana. "Better lock the car. It's a bad part of the neighborhood."

They both snickered at Lipana's witticism.

"What's the inside of the building look like?"

"It's one big room with a number of structural support beams. For all intents and purposes, there is no good place to hide in there except in a dark corner or behind one of the beams. We're entering from the south. The truck that's carrying the heroin will come in through a garage door on the west side of the building. The other teams will be entering from every possible direction on Muñoz's signal. He's got eyes on the inside."

"Your guy?"

"Nope. His guy."

As they neared the building, both Zeb and Lipana drew their weapons. The night was replete with much more than just the routine noise that accompanies a city. In the distance a dog barked mutedly but incessantly. An ambulance siren wailed nearby. A train hauling manufactured goods up from Mexico clacked across the tracks of the old Southern Railway bed. Violins, trumpets and guitars played familiar strains of Mariachi music. Hanging heavily in the air was the smell of burning incense. The irony of it being Día de Muertos, the celebration of those who had passed onto the next world, was not lost on either Zeb or Lipana. They had already gone by a half-dozen altars made by children to invite the angelitos, the spirits of dead children, to come back for a visit. Today was All-Saints day, the time when the spirits of dead adults came to visit. Tomorrow would bring All Souls Day, a Holy Day when families visited the cemeteries where their loved ones lay for all eternity. The traditional flowers of the dead, marigolds, would be placed on the graves. Oddly, the festival of the dead brought more life to the Village than just about any other celebration.

Lipana glanced at his watch. He tapped the face-plate. It was

10:44. Lipana's CI had told him the exchange, heroin for cash, was scheduled for 10:45. It was rumored that El Coyote had once been an accountant and was almost obsessively compulsive about transactions being done on time and in a professional manner.

At 10:45 the creaking strains of an industrial garage door opening filled the air. Zeb and Lipana caught each other's eye. A penetratingly intense glance was exchanged in a fraction of a second.

"When the garage door is all the way closed, we should get a go signal from Muñoz," said Lipana.

Inside the old manufacturing building the noisy sound from the compressed air of a diesel truck engine shutting down could be heard. A truck door slamming resounded throughout the building. A second door banged shut. The muted voices of men speaking in Spanish echoed in the large room behind the door where Lipana and Zeb waited anxiously. Zeb's heart began to race. A firework with a three-pronged display exploded overhead. That was the go signal from Max Muñoz. Lipana pointed to the door with his head. Zeb flung it open. Four other teams of Tucson police and police detectives simultaneously dashed into the building. Max Muñoz's voice came bulleting through a bullhorn, first in Spanish then in English.

"Todos de congelan. Everyone freeze."

The building, poorly lit to begin with, changed from shadowy darkness to pitch black. The gang had obviously prepared for this exact contingency as one of the gang members flipped the power switch to off. Bullets from automatic weapons rapidly pinged the ceiling, structural beams and walls. The contained noise was painful to everyone's ears. Zeb and Lipana stayed low, hugging the floor as they moved into a more advantageous position. The men used the support beams as best they could for cover. Bullets snapped by, striking nearby metal poles and spitting up dirt and chips of wood as they landed. Blue and orange sparks heated the tips of the firing gun barrels. Bullets pinging off steel and iron created tiny bursts of rapidly scattering light. Amidst the chaos both the police and the criminals remained amazingly calm.

"Todos de congelan. Todos de congelan. Baje las armas. Baje las armas."

The order to 'lay down your weapons' went unheeded. The sound of a diesel engine firing up filled the room. The garage door began to open slowly. Surreally, the bad guys seemed to be in no hurry whatsoever. Seeing the door opening, the Tucson policemen began firing at the truck. The driver floored the accelerator. The truck bounced off the edge of the garage door as it made a getaway into the dark of night.

"Fucking cocksuckers," said Lipana.

"What?" asked Zeb.

"They bullet-proofed the windows, doors and tires of the truck. These guys are pros."

But even as the truck vanished into the outside world, the fight inside the building was far from over. The cartel had left four men behind. They had one purpose in mind, to kill as many policemen as possible. They seemed to have no fear of death. This made them incredibly dangerous.

After a moment of quiet, the cartel assassins slipped out from their various hiding places. Bullets sprayed every corner of the building from high-powered automatic weapons. Instinctively, Zeb, who had stood behind a beam to gain a point of advantage, dove to the ground. Lipana, who should have done the same, stood his ground and fired in the direction that was most lit up from the incoming weapons. One of the automatic weapons ceased.

"Got that son of a bitch," said Lipana.

Zeb gave his partner the thumbs up, but in the next instant Zeb felt the crushing weight of Lipana's body collapsing into his back. With the pressure of Lipana's body against him, Zeb struggled for his breath. Zeb could see that Lipana had taken a round to the neck. With each dying breath, with each pump of his heart, an artery squirted blood on Zeb's face. The acrid, metallic taste and smell of a dying man's blood imprinted an unforgettable impression deep into his subconscience.

Zeb wriggled out from beneath Lipana and jumped into action.

He pressed his hand down firmly on the gaping neck wound. It did little good. He hit his two-way radio and yelled for a medic, a medic he knew would arrive too late to save his partner. Helplessness and rage shook Zeb to his very core.

When the scene cleared, two of the cartel gunmen were dead. The other two had somehow escaped, leaving their weapons in the alley. By now they blended easily into the neighborhood. One policeman had a leg injury. Lipana was gone for good.

A week later, after the hub-bub of the funeral had quelled, Zeb felt lost. His mind repeatedly asked itself a single question. Was this job worth it? Losing a partner felt far worse than how he imagined his own death would feel. In a twist of fate, the call came through that he would be bumped further up the queue toward becoming a Tucson detective. Max Muñoz advised him to take a week off.

"Take some time to think about things. Use the time to get away from it all. Straighten your head out. Go back to Safford. Get rooted. Try and remember why it is you do what you do."

Zeb hung his head. He was at the lowest point of his life. This was worse than watching the look on his mother's face when she got the news his dad was dead. Zeb's response was polite, but distant.

"Thanks, Max. That sounds like good advice."

It was more than simply good advice. It was sage counsel. Zeb's feelings were mixed, confused and literally bouncing all over the map. He called Sheriff Jake Dablo and explained what had happened. Jake listened intently. He paused for nearly a minute before responding to the young man whom he considered a son.

"Come and see me. You and I will pow-wow with Song Bird. We'll talk. Sometimes life ain't easy. Sometimes life sucks. You probably feel that it's harder to be left alive than to die."

Tears flowed from Zeb's eyes as he listened to the man he trusted most in the world. Jake understood precisely what Zeb was going through.

"Okay. I'll be there tomorrow."

"Good."

"Er, Jake?"

"Yeah?"

"Thank you."

"I know you'd do the same for me."

Zeb sat down on a nearby curb and pulled his hat over his eyes. For the first time in his life he understood that he needed help to bring him peace of mind.

19

ZEB, JAKE AND SONG BIRD

LADYBUG SADDLE

Z eb agreed to meet Jake at Earl's Tap Room near the base of Mount Graham. He asked Jake not to tell Aunt Helen he was coming home. She would spread the word too quickly and, of course, to his mother. At ten minutes before noon Jake looked at his watch. Zeb would be waiting for him at Earl's. He glanced out his window toward the parking lot that stood between his office and Mount Graham. He took a deep breath. He knew that Zeb's future could hinge on his advice. Jake grabbed his hat and walked past Helen's desk.

"I'm headed out to the Rez. I've got a meeting with Song Bird."

"Anything I need to know about?" asked Helen.

Helen's probing question was her version of being a part of the long arm of the law as well as one of the town's leading gossips.

"Mostly just a friendly visit."

Jake was little more than an open book to Helen's eyes.

"Don't lie to me, Jake Dablo. The Lord above says to tell an untruth is a transgression against His law."

"It's wrong to lie, no doubt about it," said Jake. "But I do have some important things to discuss with Song Bird."

"Is one of them my nephew?"

"What makes you ask that?"

Jake knew Helen had all the details of the shooting in Tucson. She knew that since the shooting Zeb had not called his mother. She also knew it was common practice to give an officer some time off after being involved in a circumstance in which his partner was killed.

Helen got up from her seat and walked to a west facing window. She pointed toward Mount Graham.

"It's taking everything I've got to not call Zeb. I need to talk to him. More than that I need to give him a hug. I know he needs one. But I suppose he's got a reason he's keeping distant," said Helen.

"I've walked in his shoes. He's got some things to take care of before he sees his mother. He's got to get his head on straight before he talks to her. He doesn't want to create any undue burden for her. Please respect that and let him see her on his own time."

"Is that an order?" asked Helen.

"No, it's not," replied Jake. "It's the decent thing to do. And if anyone in this office knows about doing the right thing, Helen, it is you."

Helen smiled blankly at Jake. His words danced somewhere between truth and lies. Jake could see through Helen almost as well as she could read him. He crossed his fingers, hoping that Helen would not call Marta.

Outside, Jake stepped into his vehicle and headed toward Earl's Tap. Seven minutes later he walked through the front door of the dive bar. Except for Earl, the bartender, and Zeb, the place was empty. Zeb was sitting on a stool hunched over the ancient oaken bar. A bottle of beer and a shot glass with a fifth of cheap whiskey were Zeb's true companions. He didn't even turn as Jake took a seat next to him.

"You look like shit."

"Good thing you can't see what's in my heart," mumbled Zeb.

"What am I missing?" asked Jake.

"Hatred. Straightforward disgust toward most of mankind."

Jake understood. He also knew Zeb needed to be healed in a way that Song Bird might be able to provide.

"How long are you going to feel sorry for yourself?"

Jake's words felt like a head on attack. Zeb reeled at the tone of his mentor's words.

"This ain't no pity party. This is real," said Zeb.

"You're right. It's real. It's a *real* fucking pity party."

Zeb cursed Jake under his breath. Earl slid an empty glass and a bottle of beer in front of Jake. Jake poured himself three fingers of the rot gut whiskey. Jake tipped his head back and slid the whiskey down his gullet before grabbing the beer to chase it down. Twice more he did exactly the same thing. Zeb kept up with him. For a minute or two they let the liquor settle in. It was not yet time for words.

Jake waited another minute before reaching into his pocket. He placed a twenty-dollar bill on the counter and thanked Earl. Earl tipped his head without expression or saying a word. Jake lightly but firmly placed his hand on Zeb's shoulder.

"Let's go. We've got a meeting with Song Bird."

"Where?"

"Does it matter?"

"I guess not."

"We're meeting him up on Mount Graham by Ladybug Saddle."

Outside Earl's Tap Room, Jake's truck was parked in the shade of a Shamel ash tree. Zeb got in the truck and stared out the window. Tears welled in his eyes but not from the booze. The whiskey and beer had absolutely no effect on him. Zeb had no intentions of attempting to sort out the jumble of emotions that were racking his brain. At this particular moment everything in his head was far too complicated to ponder.

The lawmen drove up the mountain in silence. Zeb had a single image in his mind. He could see nothing but the blood of his dead partner, Lipana. Zeb could see his partner's life leaving his body with each beat of his dying heart. Zeb shivered involuntarily.

On the road up Mount Graham, Jake pulled into Ladybug Saddle. Song Bird had arrived before them and built a small fire. Simply seeing Song Bird, Zeb was able to temporarily shift his focus.

"Hon dah."

As Song Bird spoke the traditional Apache greeting, he clasped Zeb by the forearm. Zeb returned the grip and the greeting. The men stared deeply into each other's eyes. The grief, along with the overwhelming desire to let his pain fly to the four winds, at once struck Zeb with immobility. Song Bird, observing with an ever-keen eye, spun Zeb around and slapped the younger man with a sharp but glancing blow between the shoulder blades. With the impact of the medicines man's hand, Zeb's consciousness shifted. The force of the blow was followed by gentle words.

"Please, come. Sit," said Song Bird, pointing to the fire.

With the overhead sun bearing down on them streaming the slopes of Mount Graham, Zeb, Song Bird and Jake stared past the flames downward into the remote wilderness of the Klondyke-Aravaipa Valley.

"What do you see?" asked Song Bird.

"Blood," replied Zeb. "Death."

The medicine man lit some sage, then quickly put it out with his fingers. With the ashes he smudged Zeb's eyes and forehead. Song Bird began to chant. The singing carried Zeb back to his childhood and the days of fishing on the San Carlos with his friends,

"There is more to the world than death and suffering," said Song Bird. "There is joy and happiness."

Silent, burning tears that seared his flesh raced down Zeb's cheeks. He could hear each tear as it landed on his cotton shirt. Once again Song Bird began to chant. Jake thumped on the drum Song Bird handed him. Zeb's tears began to burn less intensely.

Song Bird, still chanting, walked to a nearby spring and gathered several pouches of water. When he returned, Song Bird gave Zeb a command.

"Remove your clothes. All of them."

Zeb followed the medicine man's orders. His pain and being with his mentors prevented him from suffering embarrassment. Song Bird lit a second bundle of sage and danced many circles in each direction around Zeb.

"Come mighty wind," sang the medicine man. "Take away what lies on the surface. Send it to the place where it can do no harm."

An unseen hand guided Jake's drumming. It became like the wind, smooth, strong and direction oriented.

"Lay on Mother Earth."

Frozen, Zeb didn't move until Song Bird's hands gently guided him to the ground. With rocks he had earlier gathered, Song Bird surrounded the suffering son of Safford with a circle.

"May the god of the rocks protect you from violence. May he protect you from what violence does to a man," sang Song Bird. "May he lead you away from the brutality that invades your heart."

Jake's drumming changed to a simpler but stronger beat.

Song Bird rubbed herbs and plants across the skin on the front of Zeb's body. Then, he turned Zeb over and scrubbed his back with the same herbs. Lastly, he crushed the herbs onto Zeb's head and into his hair.

"Sit up," Song Bird instructed Zeb.

Using a stick with rounded head, Song Bird splashed water on Zeb. After a while he grabbed a pouch and poured water up and down Zeb's spine and over his head. It was cold, colder as the wind increased and the trees began to sway. Zeb shivered uncontrollably. Song Bird danced to divine communication with the spirits that healed those suffering from the sickness of hatred in the mind. Jake continued drumming with a force that he himself did not understand.

Song Bird took the second pouch and once again washed Zeb's body. Four times he repeated the washing process, once for each direction. Silently Song Bird prayed for the evil spirits that were compelling the evil feelings in Zeb's mind to be gone. He prayed they be replaced with peace and understanding, with love and joy, with hope.

With a nod from Song Bird, Jake stopped drumming. Song Bird neatly folded Zeb's clothes and placed them on Zeb's seated lap.

"Get dressed. It's too damn cold to be running around naked."

Zeb did as he was directed. When fully clothed, he stood. His legs were weak, but quickly his strength returned. He had the feeling of looking at the world through fresh eyes. The hatred in his heart had significantly abated. It was time to return to his duty as a detective in Tucson. But first, he needed to let his mother know he was doing okay. It was the right thing for a son to do.

20

MORALS AND TRUST

The process of becoming a Tucson police detective normally required an officer to have five years of experience. Because Tucson's population was growing rapidly it had a shortage of detectives. Zeb, with the help of Max Muñoz, was able to fast track into the position.

The background check, multiple exams, interviews and drug screening were a piece of cake. Zeb, along with the examiners, were somewhat worried about the psychological exam. Having had the recent experience of the death of his partner was an obvious and legitimate concern. Thanks to Song Bird and Jake, Zeb came through the mental review with flying colors.

A pilot program run under a federal grant obtained with the help of Senator Russell allowed for new detectives to pair up. This was a unique situation for the Tucson Police Department. As if by design, Zeb and Max Muñoz drew the same assignment. They would work together in the gang investigations detail. While this did not give them the direct duty of looking into the death of Lipana, it gave them enough latitude to follow up on leads that might be related. One day Zeb confided to Max.

"Lipana's CI got hold of me."

"Did he give you anything of value?"

"He's been underground because he was present at the shooting of Lipana. He had grown very close to Lipana. He wants Lipana's killer caught as much as we do."

"What does he want in return?" asked Max.

"He wants us to look the other way on a big pot deal that's going down tomorrow. If we do that, he'll give us a list of the people who were at the warehouse the night Lipana was killed," explained Zeb.

"How about he gives us the information first?" asked Max.

"I tried in every way to get him to agree to that, but no dice."

"Do you trust him?"

"I don't know for certain. Lipana did. I trusted Lipana. This guy never steered Lipana wrong. Yeah, I guess I trust him enough to move forward with this."

Max sighed heavily.

"Our asses are on the line if the chief of detectives finds out we are involving ourselves in Lipana's murder investigation."

"I learned a long time ago from a very smart sheriff that sometimes a man has to know how to operate just outside the lines of the law if he wants to get things done. I'm willing to take the risk. I know Lipana wasn't your partner, so if you choose not to be involved, I understand," said Zeb.

Max shook his head.

"What would you do, Zeb, if the shoe was on the other foot?"

"All things being equal, I'd help you out," replied Zeb.

"Enough said. Did the CI say what he needs the money from the pot deal for?" asked Max.

"He wants to pay a coyote to bring his grandparents across the border. They're old. They have health issues that can't be treated properly in Mexico. He wants the money to pay for the medical care as well. He's not trying to get a free government handout for them. He's going to pay for everything."

"You worked CBP. How do you feel about all that?"

"I hate coyotes. Most of them are real assholes."

"But you want your CI to pay some asshole coyote to bring his grandparents across the border?"

"It's not all that cut and dried. If the CI helps us get Lipana's killer, then I am willing to look the other way. Sometimes these kinds of things just have to be done...in the name of true justice."

Max rubbed his chin. This issue cut both ways. He knew full well there were no easy answers. On one hand, he saw the greater good possibly being served. On the other hand, what good was the law if it was not obeyed by those sworn to enforce it? Max pondered what he would want Zeb to do for him should he be killed in the line of duty. When he looked at it that way, there was no doubt he would want his killer found, if only for the sake of his own family's peace of mind.

"There's no way to get the CI to talk first? You're certain of that?"

"As certain as I'm standing here," replied Zeb.

"Fuck it. If stepping outside the law gets us Lipana's killer, then it's all good with me."

Zeb called the CI's burner phone.

"You're clear for tonight," said Zeb. "But we meet tomorrow, and we talk turkey."

"I'll give you the names after my grandparents are safely across the border," said the CI.

"Then it's a no go and you're at risk," said Zeb. "The deal you and I have is for me to look the other way on the pot deal. That, and nothing more. Comprende?"

"Okay. I had to try."

"I get it. Tomorrow. One o'clock in the parking lot at Tohonu Chul."

"Sí, sí. I'll be there."

21

TOHONU CHUL

Zeb and Max arrived an hour earlier than the scheduled meeting. Since the CI was expecting Zeb to be alone, Max went to the bistro near the La Fuente Museum gift shop to get himself a cold drink. Max parked himself on a bench beneath the shade of a small grove of palo verde trees.

Both detectives watched as tourists and locals seeking nature, art and culture pulled into the parking lot. Some took the path to the hiking trails while others headed directly to the gift shop and bistro. Zeb listened to country songs on the local radio station, KIIM 99.5. Patsy Cline's divine voice filtered through the speakers. Zeb's arm rested in the open window.

He recognized the CI's blue Silverado Chevy truck as it slowly entered the parking lot. The CI circled the lot once before pulling next to Zeb. Driving slowing but never stopping, the CI rolled down his window. As he passed close to Zeb's truck, he tossed a crumpled piece of paper through the window and slowly pulled away. Zeb uncrumpled the paper. Written down were six names. One was circled. Next to the name were the words 'trigger man'. At the bottom of the paper was a note that explained the other five men were there when the shooting happened.

Detective Max Muñoz joined his partner.

"That was brief."

"He's been in the game a long time. He knows what it takes to survive and how to do it. My guess is that he made you," said Zeb.

"What'd he give you?"

Zeb handed Max the piece of paper. Max read it carefully.

"Does the trigger man, Emilio Amador, live in Tucson?" asked Max.

"Some of the time. I got that from the CI a while ago."

"Where?"

"Out on West Valencia near Indian Agency Road."

"Let's do a drive by and check it out."

It took twenty minutes to get to Emilio Amador's neighborhood.

"Nothing unusual about his house," said Max. "It looks just like every other one in the neighborhood."

"Obviously Amador is doing his best to blend into the background and not get noticed," replied Zeb.

"It's one sign of his intelligence," replied Max.

"I suspect El Coyote has elevated Amador's stature because he killed a cop."

"In their world it proves fearlessness and machismo," said Max.

"He's also either smart enough or well-coached enough to drop off the radar."

"Like we talked about before, these guys act like players in a major corporation rather than drug thugs. The world is changing fast. We've got to keep up with them."

The pass by was the first of many. Emilio Amador was indeed crafty and clever. It would be half a year before an opportunity to nab him arose.

22

6 MONTHS LATER

"My CI's grandparents are finally completely safe and have gotten the health care they need. They are tucked away in Las Vegas, New Mexico."

"Good," replied Max. "It's time your CI came through for us in a big way."

"He just did. Take a look at this."

Zeb handed Max a photograph of the man his CI claimed was Lipana's shooter.

"Your CI give you this?"

"He did."

"When?"

"Last night."

Max scrutinized the picture.

"You're sure this is the right guy?"

"I trust it is," replied Zeb.

"You're certain this isn't some guy your CI has a vendetta against and is using us to get him?"

"I've considered that," replied Zeb. "My gut tells me we're okay. Besides, I got some more up to date information this morning."

"Do tell."

"Emilio Amador has moved a few rungs up the ladder. He's one of El Coyote's top men in human trafficking. He's picking up a group of Honduran teenage girls across the border and bringing them to Tucson."

"Why would Amador do the leg work himself?" asked Max.

"He's a hands-on type of guy and a he's a freak. I think he wants to check out the merchandise he's selling," replied Zeb. "My CI says Amador is more than a bit of a pervert."

"What's his M.O.?"

"He takes the girls to a safe house here in Tucson. He tests the merchandise over a short period of time, then sells them into prostitution in Vegas and New York. He moves them pretty quickly. Amador's gang is handling the operation."

"So, it's in our jurisdiction," added Max.

"Yup. It's right in our wheelhouse."

"The chief can't give us any grief."

"And if homicide has their shit together, with a little help from us, they should be able to directly link Amador to Lipana's murder."

Zeb and Max high-fived each other.

"When is he picking up the Honduran girls?"

"Tonight."

"Is he going to be heavily armed?" asked Max.

"According to our CI, he's not. But you never know. The CI said he'd let me know if they were going to be carrying more weapons than usual."

"How many girls?"

"A dozen."

"How many armed gang bangers?"

"Four."

"We'd better deal with the Chief directly."

"He'll want us to have enough backup."

"And he'll want to make sure the press is properly notified. I hear he's got his eyes on running for mayor."

"Let's go talk to him," said Zeb.

An hour later, joined by the head of homicide, Clark Weber, Zeb and Max were sitting in the office of the Chief of Detectives, Darvin Rambulet. Zeb detailed him in on the human trafficking that Emilio Amador of El Coyote's cartel was up to.

"This is going down tonight?" asked Chief Rambulet.

"Yes, sir," replied Zeb.

"Do you know what time?"

"Twenty-one hundred hours."

"Where?" asked Rambulet.

"Near the intersection of Twenty-second Street and Greasewood at a pink house on the southwest corner," said Zeb.

"Specific address?"

"2201 Greasewood."

"Duplex, triplex, apartment?"

"It's a freestanding house."

"I take it they're using it as a safe house?" asked Weber.

"Yes."

"We've got to get cameras up."

"How can we do that without giving ourselves away?" asked Zeb

"I'll have the city create an artificial power outage for the entire block. We can send in city utility trucks to look like they're fixing the electrical grid. Instead, they will be putting up cameras," explained Rambulet. "I want real time on this. If we can nail Lipana's killer, we can send a message to the cartel, end a long drawn out case and bring closure for Lipana's family."

Neither Zeb nor Max said it, but Chief Rambulet could have also added, 'and this will give my campaign for Mayor of Tucson a real boost.'

An hour later the city utility truck manned by undercover officers was setting up cameras on power poles up and down Greasewood Street. It was the only part of the operation that went smoothly. Weber, head of homicide, and Rambulet, chief of detectives, were both men with higher political aspirations. Both men, even before the operation began, were writing their press releases and practicing speeches for the television cameras.

"What did you say?" asked Max.

"Homicide is sending in a dozen officers and so is Rambulet," said Zeb.

"We're going to get spotted. That many officers in the vicinity might blow the whole operation."

"If it's any consolation, the detectives are acting as a perimeter. That ought to make the scene a little less crowded."

"You're certain your CI said only four of Amador's guys will be there?"

"Yup. But knowing Amador, those will be four of his best men."

One hour before the Honduran girls were due to arrive with Amador at 2201 Greasewood, Rambulet got a call from one of his field operatives.

"I might have been made," said the field op.

"What do you mean?" asked Rambulet.

"El Coyote's men, and I assume Amador's guys as well, drive new Chevy Trucks, right? With a Mexican flag somewhere on the truck?"

"Yes. Always. They all have a Mexican flag in the lower right part of the rear window."

"A green Chevy truck has circled by me three times in the last fifteen minutes. The driver and his compadre look like bad hombres."

"Could you see either the driver or the passenger's forearms?"

"Yes. The driver had his arm through the window. He has a tattoo."

"Was it a howling coyote?"

"I couldn't make that out for sure."

"Move your position. Do it in such a manner that they know what you are up to. See if they follow you. Let me know as soon as you know," said Rambulet.

Ten minutes later the field operative let the chief of detectives know he was one hundred percent certain he had been made.

"Pull out in front of them when they make their next circle around. See how far they follow you."

"Roger that."

The agent pulled out as instructed and was followed. He noticed one thing and contacted Chief Rambulet.

"I think they're bringing in reinforcements. I just saw two trucks, a red Chevy truck and a blue Chevy truck, pass by. Both had two men in them. Both had Mexican flags in the lower right rear window."

Rambulet drummed his fingers on his desk. It could be nothing at all. It could be coincidence. He called Weber, head of homicide.

"There's a pretty good possibility one of my men has been made."

"How certain are you?"

"Fairly certain. Nothing tells me they know we're coming at them."

"Fuck it," said Weber. "This is as close as we're going to get to Amador. He's been getting away with this shit for too god-damned long. Send a message to your men. Tell them to be on ultra-high alert status. I'll do the same with mine."

Rambulet contacted his men. So did Weber. What neither man knew was that they were being set up. Somehow, the cartel had access to all of Tucson's police communications. Things were about to go south for Zeb and Max.

At twenty-one hundred hours, right on time, Amador arrived with the twelve Honduran teenage girls. At twenty-one-ten the dozen officers were in their assigned positions. At twenty-one-fifteen the operation went into effect.

Outside the house on Greasewood, Max and Zeb separated. Max covered the southeast corner of the house. Zeb stuck his head near a large, open window on the south side of the house. A single shot rang out. It hit Max in the leg. He crawled behind a row of dense weigela bushes for cover. Out of nowhere, a giant-sized Mexican thug grabbed Zeb around the neck and held a gun to his head.

"Don't make a fucking move, cowboy. If you do, it'll be your last one."

His English was clear, but the breath of the man speaking into Zeb's ear smelled of rancid pork, chilis, vinegar and ammonia. Zeb knew he was dealing with a meth head. The brute's next words had Zeb suspecting he was Amador's personal bodyguard. From the corner of his right eye, Zeb could see the Honduran girls and only two other men with weapons. Standing directly next to the man who had the odiferous breath was Amador. Zeb recognized him instantly.

Amador stepped through the window. He jammed his gun in Zeb's ribs.

"Don't move an inch if you value your life."

The bodyguard followed Amador out the window. Seconds later the meth head bodyguard had his gun shoved into Zeb's kidneys.

"How many of you are there?" asked Amador.

When Zeb didn't respond, Amador pulled a knife and held it under Zeb's left nostril. One push of the knife and it would be planted deep inside Zeb's brain. The old adage about discretion being the greater part of valor hung over Zeb like the Sword of Damocles.

"Six."

"Are they after me?" asked Amador.

"No. Not you."

"Who, then?"

"The girls. The prostitution squad got a tip."

There was no prostitution squad per se. Dealing with underage prostitutes involved a dozen cross-agency interactions. Zeb had no mind to discuss the details of all that with a gun pointed at his ribs.

Amador was too used to people fearing him. He believed Zeb. It made sense. Amador shouted in Spanish to someone in the house.

"Abra la puerta de entrada. Deja salir a las chicas."

From Zeb's elementary understanding of Spanish, he knew Amador was instructing one of his men to let the girls out the front door.

"Smart move," said Zeb. "If the prostitution squad has the girls, you might just get out of here in one piece."

"Shut the fuck up, vaquero. You're my ticket out of here. Tucson police don't shoot their own. They only shoot Mexicanos de pieles marrones and hombres negros."

In the shadows beneath the weigela bush Zeb could see Max laying on his belly. The tip of his firearm was aimed directly in his direction. He was only fifty feet away. All the bragging Max had done and the ridiculous stories he told about his shooting abilities came to mind—how he could clip the head off a ten-penny nail at a hundred yards or wing a house fly in mid-flight at fifty feet came. Zeb prayed Max had been telling the truth.

Amador sneaked in behind his thug, the man who had a gun uncomfortably poking Zeb in the side.

"We've got your man," shouted Amador. "Unless you want to take home a corpse, you'd better let us get the hell out of here."

Before anyone had a chance to answer, four shots rang out from Max's gun. The first shot removed the weapon and a couple of fingers from the hand of the bad-breathed thug. The second round blasted the thug in the lungs. He fell to his knees, gasping for air. Zeb dove for the dirt. Amador, in shock, stood dumbstruck. As he raised his weapon, Max shot him through the heart...twice.

Officers emerged from everywhere. A medic tended to Max. Another officer who had been trained as a medic checked out Zeb. The lieutenant on the scene barked orders. In no time the crime scene was taped off, the Honduran girls were being processed and Max was on his way to the hospital, Zeb at his side.

"How are you feeling, hot shot?"

"The leg hurts. I hope I don't end up with a limp. Man, I'd hate to hobble through life. A bum leg would make me a desk jockey. No way that works for me."

"By the way, thanks for saving my life."

"All in a day's work."

"I guess you weren't kidding about your shooting skills."

"Being proficient with a firearm is not something a boy from Double Adobe kids about."

Max and Zeb laughed and high fived each other. As they sat there in a moment of quiet, the mood changed.

"Tonight got me thinking," said Zeb.

"About what?" asked Max.

"Home."

"Yeah, days like this can make you long for the peace of Safford or Double Adobe."

Zeb got really quiet. Max could practically see his partner's mind churning.

"Are you thinking about quitting the force?" asked Max.

"Sheriff Dablo called last night and offered me a job."

"You miss home?"

"Some. More than that, I don't think I'm cut out for the big city."

Max reached up and flipped back Zeb's cowboy hat.

"I hear you, my friend. Some of us belong in small towns and others of us belong in the big city. I think you know where you belong."

"I do."

They rode in silence to the emergency room. Zeb stayed with Max until they got him ready for surgery.

"You gonna turn in your resignation?" asked Max.

"I'm going to sleep on it. Then I'll have a little chat with the chief. When I've done that I'm going to talk with Sheriff Dablo and my old friend Song Bird."

"The medicine man."

"Right."

"You have to do what's right for you. We all only got one ride on this merry-go-round called life," said Max. "You've got to make the most of it."

"Good luck in surgery."

"Piece of cake," replied Max. "I had my tonsils out when I was six, and I got to eat ice cream for a week."

The men laughed, but both carried sadness in their eyes. Zeb and Max knew their partnership was over. Zeb was headed home to Safford.

THE END

NATIVE ROOTS READING GUIDE

This novella, NATIVE ROOTS, is a 2-part mystery. Part I takes place when Zeb Hanks is 13 years old, approximately 30 years ago. It is written to give the reader insight into Zeb's philosophy, developmental point of view and how he becomes interested in a career as a law man. Part I also shows the reader some of Zeb's early influences, both good and bad, and how he learns that a person can do the wrong thing for the right reason. A glimpse into Zeb's early understanding of Song Bird's mystical ways is shown. Some of the characters introduced in Part I are maintained throughout the entire series. The main idea is to allow you, the current readers, potential readers and future readers of the ZEB HANKS: Small Town Sheriff Big Time Trouble series, insight into how Zeb is influenced by the world, how his personal and family interactions affect him and, ultimately, the fundamental roots of who he was as a youth on the verge of becoming a man. Hence the title, NATIVE ROOTS.

In Part II we see Zeb as he is developing into a lawman. Zeb has graduated from Safford High School and taken a job at the Danforth-Roerg Copper Company. With the summer ending and his friends going off to college, Zeb chooses to become a United States Border Patrol (CBP) agent. The reader gets a brief view of his time as a border patrol agent and more time as a Tucson policeman/detective. Zeb is introduced to the jaded world of politics and law enforcement. Troublesome circumstances, what he learns about how the system operates and what happens to him ultimately lead him back home to Safford, AZ.

This novella is for new readers and for readers who want to know more about Zeb's background. In essence, it is two short mysteries that show Zeb at two stages of his life prior to becoming Sheriff of Graham County. I feel it is important for the readers to understand Zeb's personal development, how he develops friendships, what makes him tick, what makes him who he is. I add many other background details that allow the readers to understand Zeb's personal insights. Most of all I want the reader to know that, like all of us, Zeb is flawed. His imperfections, mistakes and development help him become the man he is in the ongoing series: ZEB HANKS: Small Town Sheriff Big Time Trouble.

Thanks to all of you for reading, reviewing, telling others, etc., about the ZEB HANKS mystery series. If you enjoyed it, please tell others about it, share on your FB, websites, and other social media platforms. I would like to have you help me make the ZEB HANKS series a bestseller and perhaps even a TV show. To do that I need you all to help me spread the word. Thanks again. And, as Zeb says, "It's a good idea to obey the law."

ALSO BY MARK REPS

ZEB HANKS MYSTERY SERIES

NATIVE BLOOD

HOLES IN THE SKY

ADIÓS ÁNGEL

NATIVE JUSTICE

NATIVE BONES

NATIVE WARRIOR

NATIVE EARTH

NATIVE DESTINY

NATIVE TROUBLE

NATIVE ROOTS (PREQUEL NOVELLA)

THE ZEB HANKS MYSTERY SERIES 1-3

AUDIOBOOK

NATIVE BLOOD

HOLES IN THE SKY

ADIÓS ÁNGEL

OTHER BOOKS

BUTTERFLY (WITH PUI CHOMNAK)

HEARTLAND HEROES

ABOUT THE AUTHOR

Mark Reps has been a writer and storyteller his whole life. Born in small-town southeastern Minnesota, he trained as a mathematician and chiropractor but never lost his love of telling or writing a good story. As an avid desert wilderness hiker, Mark spends a great deal of time roaming the desert and other terrains of southeastern Arizona. A chance meeting with an old time colorful sheriff led him to develop the Zeb Hanks character and the world that surrounds him.

To learn more, check out his website www.markreps.com, his AllAuthor profile, or any of the profiles below. To join his mailing list for new release information and more click here.

BB bookbub.com/authors/mark-reps

f facebook.com/ZebHanks

𝕎 twitter.com/markreps1

9 781796 553147